THE BOY *from* SEVILLE

THE BOY *from*
SEVILLE

Dorit Orgad

Translated from the Hebrew by Sondra Silverston

Illustrations by Avi Katz

Kar-Ben Publishing Minneapolis

Kar-Ben Publishing
A division of Lerner Publishing Group, Inc.
241 First Avenue North
Minneapolis, MN 55401 U.S.A.

Website address: www.lernerbooks.com

Library of Congress Cataloging-in-Publication Data

Orgad, Dorit.
    [Na'ar mi-Sivilyah English]
    The boy from Seville / by Dorit Orgad ; translated from the Hebrew by
Sondra Silverston.
        p.   cm.
    Summary: At age eleven, Manuel has already fled with his family from
Portugal to Spain because the seventeenth-century persecution of Jews is less
severe there, but passing as Christian becomes more and more difficult as the
Inquisition continues.
    ISBN: 978-1-58013-253-4 (lib. bdg. : alk. paper)
    1. Jews—Spain—History—Juvenile fiction. 2. Inquisition—Spain—Juvenile
fiction. [1. Jews—Spain—History—Fiction. 2. Inquisition—Spain—Fiction.
3. Prejudices—Fiction. 4. Spain—History—Philip III, 1598–1621—Fiction.]
    I. Silverston, Sondra. II. Title.
    PZ7.O63185Boy 2007
    [Fic]—dc22   2006009624

Manufactured in the United States of America
1 2 3 4 5 6 – BP – 12 11 10 09 08 07

Chapter One
WHAT CHANGED AFTER A LONG NIGHTTIME CONVERSATION

We're new in the city, but I already know my way around pretty well. And today, when my father sent me out on an errand for him, I had the chance to show it.

Actually, he didn't ask me to go. I volunteered. I heard Mother say to Father that our servant was sick, so we should start preparing for the Sabbath today—we never let the servants see what we do on the Sabbath and Jewish holidays. Everyone thinks we're pure Christians, and heaven help us if they ever find out we're not.

We keep chickens in the yard, and when the servants can't see, Father takes one to the home of Don Anton Martinez. There, in a hidden place in his courtyard, Don Anton slaughters the chicken according to Jewish rules.

Our relatives, who've been living in this city for a long time, showed Father and me how to find the home of Don Anton and told us that we had to be very careful. You put the chicken that's going to be slaughtered in a sack and make sure it's completely hidden. And, of course, you don't tell anyone where you're going or why. You can only go into the courtyard if you see the agreed upon sign in the window—five flowerpots. If there are only four, you leave and come back later.

At first, my parents couldn't decide whether to let me take the chicken to Don Anton. They kept asking if I knew the way, and if I knew how to hide the chicken, and if I knew about the flowerpots. Finally, they agreed to let me do it, because my father—who's a doctor—had to go to treat a duke and visit other patients, and he didn't know whether he'd be back before evening.

Mother put the cackling chicken into a sack, and I hid it under my tunic. "Just make sure you keep quiet in there," I told the chicken silently. And to my parents I said, "Don't worry, everything will be fine." I could see in their eyes that they were proud of me, but worried about me as well. I left quickly before they could change their minds.

Two hours later, I was on my way out of Don Anton Martinez's courtyard with the slaughtered chicken hidden in the sack under my tunic. At least I didn't have to worry about its cackling anymore!

"Go quickly," Don Anton Martinez urged me, "And don't stop anywhere!"

"I know," I said.

I was so happy that I felt as if I were walking on air. I'd carried out my mission perfectly and I'd be home soon. Mother would pluck the chicken quickly, and I'd bury the feathers in the ground. Even though I wanted to run, I made myself walk slowly. If you run in the street, you make people curious. I walked as if I weren't in a hurry to get anywhere, and I looked straight ahead.

"Hey, you," I heard someone call, and I knew he meant me.

"Look at that Portuguese," a voice said, and then I turned around and saw a gang of boys in the courtyard I'd just passed. They were looking at me curiously, but there was also something threatening in their eyes.

I wondered how they knew just by glancing at me that I was from Portugal. I was afraid, because for them, the Portuguese and the New Christians (*cristianos nuevos*) are the same. I knew it would not be a good idea to stop, so I started walking faster.

"Wait," a strong voice ordered me, and other voices joined it. "Wait."

I wanted to run away, but I stood my ground. I was afraid that the boys would chase me all the way home, and I didn't want them to know where I lived. My heart was pounding wildly. But I stood there and faced them.

"A Portuguese, right?" asked a boy who was probably the leader of the gang. I recognized his strong voice as the one who'd first called out to me.

I nodded and turned to walk away.

"Stand still," the same boy ordered me. "What's your name?"

"Manuel . . ."

"I could see right away that he's one of the *cristianos nuevos*," one of the boys said jeeringly, and added with hatred, "*Judaizante.*"

"No," I protested, "That's not true!"

"Don't lie, Manuel!" the gang leader rebuked me. "All the Portuguese here are New Christians, and you're all really Jews."

"That's a lie," I said. "I'm not a *judaizante*. I'm a Christian like you. Oh Holy Mary," I said, looking upward. "I have to go."

"First let's see what you have there," the leader of the gang said as he came over to me. "There, under your *capa*." He tried to lift my tunic.

The only thing I can do now is run, I thought. But what would happen if they caught up to me? And running away is like admitting you're guilty.

I had no idea what to do, and I was so scared that I almost fainted. But then I heard a voice that seemed to come from inside me, not my own voice—and certainly not the dead chicken's! It said to me, "Don't be afraid, Manuel, stand up straight and show them how broad your shoulders are. Take a step forward and tell that boy it's none of his business."

I did what that inner voice told me, and the boys looked at me in amazement. In the silence, I could hear the beating of my heart. But the feeling of power left me as suddenly as it had come upon me and I started to be afraid again.

The boys must have sensed this. They moved closer to me, and the one who'd first called me *"judaizante"* took a deep breath and came up to me with his chest puffed out. "Show us what you have under your *capa*," he said, staring at me with hatred in his eyes.

"He probably stole something," one of the boys said.

I shook my head emphatically. I couldn't say a word. My tongue was stuck to the roof of my mouth.

Just then, we heard the sound of galloping horses, and we turned to look at the horsemen who were riding

through the alley. I heard that same inner voice order me: "Now's your chance. Run as fast as you can and don't look back."

I didn't run toward home. I turned around and raced back in the direction of Don Anton Martinez's courtyard. I didn't stop. I just kept running.

The boys chased me, yelling, "Thief, Portuguese thief! Catch him!"

It was so hot in Seville that day that the streets were practically empty and no one stopped me. The sweat dripping from my forehead blurred my vision. I could not see where I was going. And I didn't dare look back.

I ran as fast as I'd ever run before—not an easy thing to do with a chicken swinging from side to side in a sack under your tunic!

I didn't stop until I got to the river. Everything seemed to be whirling around in front of me, but I realized that it was my own panic that was making me feel like everything was topsy-turvy. When a little time had passed and I saw that the boys who had been chasing me were nowhere to be seen, I calmed down a bit.

I sat down under a tree not far from the large river, the Guadalquivir. I felt the need to say a prayer of thanks. Not out loud, of course, but in my heart I gave thanks to God, the God of the Jews, the God that I had felt existed even before my father talked to me about Him. I don't know how or why, but I suddenly felt strong again, and I knew that even if those boys showed up now, I wouldn't be afraid of them anymore.

I remembered the night my father told me that we weren't Christians, as I had thought until then—the night my whole life turned completely around. The things he told me that night opened the door to a new world for me, a majestic world that was wonderful and awe-inspiring at the same time. From that night on, I'd been waiting for the chance to prove to my parents that I deserved the trust they'd put in me.

The evening had begun with a big meal, and then I had gone down to the cellar with Father and we talked almost till dawn. Sitting down there in the candlelight, Father began, "Manuel, I hope you have eaten your fill. Because we will fast until tomorrow night."

Then he explained that we were not Christians as I had been brought up to believe, but that we were Jews. He talked for many hours about who we were and what we believe and why we must keep our beliefs a secret. He told me why Jews fast on Yom Kippur, and I was proud that he was going to let me fast too.

Now that I knew we were Jews, so many things made sense to me.

Born in 1622, I was just a little kid when we fled from our home in Bragança, Portugal, to Spain, but I always wondered why we left. We didn't come straight here, to Seville. At first, we were in the capital, Madrid.

How I suffered in that big city. The children used to bully us for reasons I didn't understand, me and my little brother Juan, who is four years younger than I am. All they had to do was see us and they'd start yelling: "Dirty Portuguese." And they called us even worse things—*marranos* and *sucios*.

Juan didn't want to go outside because of them. But our small apartment in Madrid was so crowded that we could hardly move. We had to go outside sometimes.

One day, Remedios, our big sister, went to buy something in the market. Juan went with her and she held his hand the whole time. But when her hands were full of vegetables and Juan had to hold onto her dress, he lost his grip and they lost each other in the crowd.

The market was close to where we lived, and Juan could have found the way back by himself. But he was terrified and started to cry. In an instant, a crowd of people and children were standing around him. They asked him why he was crying, and when he didn't answer, a man, who was with his two children, forced him to go home with them.

In the man's house, they gave him a piece of cake and begged him to calm down. They said to little Juan, "We're your friends. Don't be afraid of us."

Juan wasn't afraid of them. But he wouldn't talk to them. He just sat there and didn't say a word.

They said, "We know your family. You're from Portugal, *cristianos nuevos*."

Juan kept silent, and then the man said, "We'll take you home, and tomorrow we'll come to your courtyard—so you can play with the children."

And they brought him home. Juan told us all that, but in a mixed-up way, and I tried to make sense out of what he said. Because what he told us was very important.

It seems that we were very lucky that Juan had refused to speak. If he had spoken, we might have gotten into a lot of trouble. The man who took my little brother to his house had been waiting to latch onto a lost child in the market. He worked with the

Inquisition, and his specialty was to get children to talk and say incriminating things about their families.

We found out that other Portuguese children had been caught in his net, and after they chattered away—the way young children do—their parents were taken to the Inquisition cellars to be interrogated. It was enough for a child to say that his family dipped their hands in water before eating, and they would be accused of observing Jewish customs.

I saw that man when he came to our house with his children to wait for Juan. He looked like a nice person, and I wasn't surprised that he was so good at his job. They say that's the devil's way, to come disguised as a "good fellow" who only wants the best for you. He came a few times to trap Juan, and if we hadn't moved to Seville, maybe he would have succeeded.

Here I am, getting carried away in the flood of my memories when I'm still in the middle of telling the story of what happened when I left Don Anton Martinez's courtyard. As I sat under the tree, I thought about my sister, Remedios, who would probably be very glad to hear about what I'd done.

Remedios didn't know that they'd allowed me to go to have the chicken slaughtered. She'd left the house early in the morning to help Aunt Tereza prepare for the Sabbath. If she'd been home, maybe she'd have objected to my going. Still, sitting under the tree, I thought about how she always worries that something bad might happen to me or Juan. Now, when she comes home, she'll find out that I really can be trusted. What I'd done would prove to her that I'm a grown-up.

Chapter Two
Aldino and the Black Sheep of the Family

I was still sitting under the tree feasting my eyes on the blue river, starting to feel calm and relaxed. The tree had widespread branches that kept out the blazing sunlight, and the darkness almost lulled me to sleep.

In the quiet, I could hear the buzzing of flies, which were the most alert of all creatures on such a hot day, and I was busy shooing them away.

Suddenly the loud, clear bleat of a sheep made me jump. I hadn't seen it crouching under a bush. The sheep kept on bleating as if it were calling someone. I came out of my hiding place under the tree and went to see if there was anyone around on the theory that it would be better to find him before he found me!

The black sheep was tied to the trunk of a bush with a rope. How could that be, I wondered. Anybody passing by could take that sheep for himself.

I remembered the lamb we used to eat in Bragança. I didn't know then that it was in honor of the Jewish holiday that celebrated the exodus from Egypt. I learned that when my father and I talked in the cellar.

The black sheep was very big, and I thought it had

enough meat to feed my family and all of our relatives in Seville for a whole week! But it was not mine, and taking it would be stealing.

I looked all around again, and there was no one. I went back to my hiding place under the tree and thought about what to do: go back home—I knew my mother was worrying about me—or to wait a while longer just to be sure that I wouldn't run into those boys who chased me.

If I left the slaughtered chicken here, I could go home and not be afraid that those boys would come after me. But where could I hide it? The smell would attract dogs and other animals to the place, and they'd find it even if I dug a hole in the ground and buried it.

I was frightened. Who knows what was waiting for me in the narrow streets that led to my home? And what if the boys went to get the *guardas*? I had just had one very scary encounter with the *guardas* when they came to our house last Saturday.

"Is your house always so clean?" one of them had asked after his eyes had examined every single corner.

"Yes, sir," Father replied. "My wife insists on having a clean house. She enjoys spending all her time scrubbing and polishing," Father said jokingly.

The tall man did not smile. The look he gave us was suspicious, jeering, and resentful.

"And do you always have a white tablecloth on your table," he asked, continuing his interrogation. "Is there by any chance some connection between what I see in your house and the seventh day of the week?"

"No connection, I swear by the Holy Mother, sir!"

I admired my father for that ability of his to put on an act, as if the policeman had absolutely no reason to be suspicious, as if the house really didn't look different on the Sabbath.

But the faces of my mother and of Remedios were white as ghosts, and I was scared. Only little Juan, who didn't know our secret, kept on running around the house, making a commotion. I wanted to make him stop, but my father motioned for me to let him be. After the policemen left, Father told me that my brother's playfulness helped him get through the awkward moments.

The policemen didn't come to our house accidentally. Maybe someone suspected us, and what if my being discovered with the chicken added to those suspicions? If the boys really did call the policemen now and they found me headed home on a Friday afternoon with a specially slaughtered chicken, they'd most certainly accuse us of observing the Torah of Moses.

Father told me what they do to *judaizantes*, to Jewish converts. They burn them at the stake! First they make them suffer by torturing them and then . . . No, I'd better not dwell on that.

What I had to do now was think, think carefully and not make any mistakes. How stupid it was to ask them to let me take the chicken to be slaughtered. I'm only a child—why didn't I think about the possibility that boys I met on the way might gang up on me? I was lucky to escape them. But what'll happen if I go back? Wouldn't it be better to leave the slaughtered chicken here?

Mother would feel bad. She saves all week for the Sabbath. Father still doesn't earn much money, and we have to make do with very little. Because of me, the Sabbath dinner would be as meager as the meals we eat during the week.

Thinking about food made me very hungry. No, I said to myself, I won't throw away this chicken—I'll hide it somewhere and later I'll come back with Father to get it. But Father said he'd be busy today. Remedios wasn't home, and Mother couldn't walk far because she had problems with her legs.

My stomach rumbled. I have to go home, I thought. I'll hide the chicken and come back tonight to get it. Where can I hide it so the animals can't get at it? I'll hang it on a high branch. Dogs, foxes, and jackals can't climb trees.

My eyes traveled up the tree until they suddenly stopped, along with my heart. I was so scared that I stopped breathing. High in the tree, right above me, someone was lying perfectly still on a wide branch.

I let out a scream and the branch moved. I saw the frightened face of a boy my age, staring at me with fear in his black eyes.

When I saw how scared he was, my own fear disappeared. "Come down," I ordered him, trying to keep my voice from shaking. "Come down right now!"

The boy didn't move.

"If you don't come down, I'll climb up!" I warned him.

"I'm coming down," the boy said in a rough voice, and in a few seconds, he slid down the trunk, landing in front of me. I was most relieved to see that he was shorter and skinnier than I was.

"Don't be afraid," I told him. "If you tell me the truth, I won't hurt you."

The boy looked at me with his frightened black eyes.

"What's your name?"

"Aldino."

"What are you doing here?"

"I came with my sheep . . ."

"That black sheep is yours?"

Aldino nodded.

"What were you doing on the tree?"

"I was hiding. I saw you running here. I didn't know what you wanted."

I believed him. "All right, you can take your sheep and go."

"Thank you," Aldino said, giving me a strange bow. Then he walked back to the bush where the sheep was bleating.

"Wait," I called, "who are you?" I had the feeling that he wasn't an ordinary Sevillian boy.

"I told you, my name is Aldino," he replied in a scared voice, as if he were afraid of what I would do.

"A Christian?"

"What else," the boy said defensively, and then added as if he were apologizing, "I'm a *morisco*."

"*Morisco*?" I repeated, and then I remembered that *moriscos* were Moors who had converted to Christianity.

"Don't think that we're slaves," the boy continued in a clear voice. "We were once, but not anymore. My father is a sandal maker—a *borceguinero*. We have our own house and a sheep. My mother makes very good cheese from the sheep's milk. Do you want to taste some?

Here, I have a piece in my bag."

Aldino gave me bread and cheese, and they melted in my mouth. I don't think I ever tasted anything so delicious. I was grateful to the strange boy for sharing his meal with me, and I wanted to repay him.

"If you come to my house with me, I'll give you some honey cake my mother baked," I said to him.

"I've never been in anybody's house outside our neighborhood, where only *moriscos* live. We stay to ourselves and don't mix with other people," Aldino said, adding, "I always wanted to see how people who are not *moriscos* live."

"Will you come with me?"

"What about the sheep?"

"I'll go with you to take her home, and then you'll come to my house with me," I suggested, very pleased with my plan. I was actually thinking that God sent this boy to me to get me out of here with my chicken.

Aldino saw the sack I shoved under my tunic, but he didn't ask any questions. We walked slowly, because of the sheep, and I told him about Madrid, the big city Aldino had never been to. I told him about my family, and I made a point of saying that we were faithful *cristianos*. Father told me that I had to use every opportunity to make people think we were *cristianos*, but without exaggerating, because that might make them suspicious.

I told Aldino that we went to church to pray every Sunday, that we ate the holy bread, and all the rest. But he didn't seem to be interested, so I talked about other things. I saw that he was interested in my father's work as a doctor, so I told him how he cured Father Miguel, the priest in the San Juan Church in Portugal.

Father Miguel had been very sick, and no one thought he would recover and go back to working as a priest. My father was the only doctor in Bragança who refused to give up and kept treating him until he got well.

"Why did you and your family leave Portugal?" Aldino asked.

I couldn't tell him the truth. I wanted him to think of me as a pure Christian, so all I said was, "We came to Spain because our whole family is here."

"Your whole family is here, in Seville?" Aldino asked.

I didn't know how to answer him. I nodded so he'd be satisfied and wouldn't ask any more questions. But I felt very uncomfortable.

No one seemed to know where my Uncle Alonso was. A month ago, after the man who used to be his servant gave testimony in the *Santo Oficio*, Uncle Alonso vanished from the city. To this day, we haven't seen or heard from him. My Aunt Catalina, Alonso's wife, worries about him constantly. And their children are very sad. Yesterday, when they came to visit, I tried to talk to my cousin Fernando, who is two years older than I am. We had always been friends, but this time he would hardly speak to me.

"Over there," Aldino said, pointing to a group of run-down huts, "that's where I live."

Chapter Three
A Secret Message

I hid my feelings about how shabby Aldino's house looked and put on a happy face. Aldino's house consisted of one room that had mats and some large pots in it. It pained me to see the poverty that showed on the thin faces of the people who lived there. It amazed me that he hadn't thought twice about giving me some of his cheese and a piece of the one slice of bread he had with him.

The sheep slept right next to the mat where Aldino and his big brother slept, and I asked him if she didn't wake them up at night.

"She doesn't start bleating until the sun comes up," Aldino replied, petting the sheep's back. "She's a good sheep. We get a lot of good milk from her."

Aldino told his mother that he was going with me, and we walked toward my neighborhood. Before we even reached my house, I could see my mother standing at the window, and my heart started to pound. When Juan saw us coming, he ran out and said, "Mother is so worried, she doesn't know what to do. Who's with you, Manuel?"

"This is Aldino, my friend," I said and walked quickly into the house.

I asked myself what was going through my mother's mind and what she thought of me. I wasn't even going to be able to explain what happened—not in front of Aldino. I went inside and the only thing I said was, "I'm sorry I'm late, Mother. Meet Aldino. He's a *morisco* and his father is a *borceguinero*."

"That's good," my mother said, without showing what she was feeling. "My sandals need to be repaired."

"I'll take them now and return them right after my father fixes them," Aldino said happily.

"I only have one pair..."

"I'll ask him to fix them today," Aldino said, grabbing the sandals from where they lay and running out the door.

"Wait, eat something first, have something to drink," I called after him, but he didn't stop.

When he was gone, my mother's expression changed, and she let out all the feelings she'd been keeping inside. "I was pulling out my hair with worry. How could you do this? And we thought you were grown-up already! We trusted you! Don't we have enough to worry about? Did you have to add this, Manuel?" she cried in fury.

I opened my mouth to reply, but she wouldn't let me, and kept on scolding me. "How could you go and make friends with boys from the street without even thinking that you could get caught carrying the chicken? Do you know what could happen to your father? We haven't heard anything about your uncle for

thirty days, and you want the same thing to happen to your father, because of you? Don't you have a brain in your head?"

When she finally let me talk, I told Mother about what had happened that morning, and she bit her lips as she listened.

"I'm sorry, Manuel dear," she said, and hugged me. I think she felt that I had handled things well—although I wasn't quite sure.

That evening, when my father came home from visiting his patients and heard what had happened, he said, "We have to be even more careful than usual now. Alonso's disappearance after being detained for questioning puts our whole family in danger. A reckless act or an unnecessary word from one of us might lead to interrogations in the cellars of *Santo Oficio*.

"We are all responsible for what happened today. It wasn't wise to send Manuel to the slaughterer's courtyard. And we must give thanks to our God, the God of our forefathers, for being with the boy in his hour of need and making sure his pursuers didn't catch him.

"I hope, Manuel, that you were careful about what you said to the shoemaker's son. Even though he is a *morisco* and they are almost as persecuted as we are, we can't trust him and his people.

"Think about Alonso. Even though it was his Christian servant and not the *moriscos* who gave him up to the Inquisition, there are many *moriscos* working as servants in wealthy homes, and it is the way of servants to spread rumors."

"Aldino's father isn't a servant," I cried.

"I know, my son. But we must be careful of every-one, both the Christians and the Muslims."

"Were the *moriscos* Muslims?" I asked, because I didn't know much about them, only that they had con-verted to Christianity and that they had once ruled Spain.

"The Moors who remained Muslims after the Christians took over the country were deported from Spain, like the Jews. The ones who stayed converted to Christianity and they are New Christians, like us," my father said, confirming what I knew.

Now I had another question. "You told me that the Jews in Portugal didn't decide to become Christian. You said that we were forced to become Christian against our will."

"Yes, that's true. We were forced to act like Christians even though in our hearts we remained faithful to the religion of our forefathers all these years. I was fortunate enough to have learned the Torah of Moses from my grandfather. You, my son, have no grandfather to teach you, so I have taken it upon my-self to do so. When you grow up and marry and have children, Manuel, you will pass on to them the princi-ples of our holy religion."

"No, Father, you will!" I cried.

"God willing," he said, and looked up at the sky. "But lately I have been feeling like a thousand eyes are following me everywhere I go. We can't know what the future holds for us. I think that the ground is burning under our feet."

"Maybe we should have stayed in Madrid," Mother

27

said as if she were talking to herself. "If we had stayed there, what happened to Alonso wouldn't have put us in so much danger."

Father laughed, but without any happiness. "Oh, dear Ines, you are as naive as a little girl. The Institution of the Holy Inquisition has spread its net over all of Spain. It doesn't matter what city we live in. Sooner or later, they would find out that I am Alonso Nuñez's brother and that you are the cousin of his wife, Catalina. They would find us wherever we are.

"Do you remember how, in Bragança, they first caught your relative, Julio, and then they arrested his family in Lisbon and in other cities."

"That was in Portugal, Rodrigo," Mother said.

"And that's why there is no trace of that family left." Father said. "Here in Seville, at least, they are not in such a hurry to burn New Christians at the stake. Have you forgotten what happened in Madrid in 1632? Have you forgotten the public trials they called 'The Torments of Christ?' How the Inquisition caught Portuguese, accused them of being Jews, and falsely charged them with whipping crucifixes? And how did these people end up? They were burned at the stake in an *auto de fe.*"

"You're telling me this as if I don't remember it," Mother said. "That whole ridiculous story of *conversos* whipping Jesus on the cross spread throughout the world, and everyone talked constantly about Jesus appearing and asking, 'Why do you torture me?' And those poor people were burned at the stake because of that slanderous lie! And yet we thought that here, in

Spain, we could live quietly," Mother said with a sigh.

"How could we know that what happened to Alonso would happen at the very time we arrived here? After all, he was highly respected in the city. They almost appointed him a *regidor*. It was only because his servant, Sancho, informed on him that he did not become a member of the City Council," Father said.

"What did that Sancho say? What was his testimony?" Mother asked.

Father shrugged. "We can't know anything until Alonso is actually arrested and they read the indictment to him."

We were still talking when my sister Remedios and my Aunt Tereza came in.

"You have such a wonderful daughter," my aunt praised my sister to my parents. "She has hands of gold. Look, we brought only some of the food we cooked today. We'll take the rest from my house on Sunday, when we go out into the country."

My aunt was interrupted by Juan's voice calling from outside. "Manuel, your friend's on his way."

I went to meet Aldino, who was panting at the door.

"I ran almost the whole way. It's frightening to be outside at night. Here are your sandals, Señora," he said, handing my mother her sandals, which had been repaired.

"Thank you, my boy. How much does your father charge for his work?"

"Three *meravedis*," Aldino said, and turned his black eyes to the floor.

My father paid him, and my mother invited him to

sit down at the table. "Manuel told us that he promised you some honey cake," she said, and my friend blushed. "I've already eaten," he said. "I'm not hungry."

"No," I cried. "You won't leave here without eating with us. You promised!"

Aldino looked around, embarrassed. "What a beautiful house you have," he whispered as he sat down next to me.

"You think *this* is a beautiful house," Juan bragged. "It's a shanty compared to the house we had in Bragança. There we were rich, and here we're poor!"

A look from my father stopped my little brother's wagging tongue, and he closed his mouth.

Aldino ate very little of the food my mother served, and when she put the wine on the table, he recoiled. My father understood and said, "Children don't drink wine."

"But I . . ." Juan burst out, and shut up again when he saw that look in my father's eyes.

After the meal, my father and I walked Aldino home. On the way home, my father said to me, "Muslims are not allowed to drink wine."

"But Aldino said he's Christian."

"We also say we're Christians, Manuel. But if you are ever in the kind of situation Aldino was in at our table, don't let anyone find out your secret, even if you are served pork, which we are forbidden to eat.

"Just today, when I was in the Duke's home and they served me wine in a cup that someone had drunk from after eating pork, I drank without blinking an eye.

"No one must ever find out our secret, Manuel. Our

lives depend on it!"

As we walked, I saw that Father was turning off the road that led to our house.

"Where are we going, Father?"

"To the home of my friend, Melchor Pereira. Someone is waiting for us there."

"Who?"

"A man I don't know. He stopped me today at the Duke's door and told me that he had something for me. We agreed to meet tonight. I told him to go to the Pereiras' home and not to our house or to any of our relatives' houses, because they are being watched by people from the *Santo Oficio*."

"Are you saying that they are constantly watching us and our relatives?"

"I think so. Ever since Alonso disappeared, I've been seeing people wandering around our house and around Aunt Tereza's house and Aunt Catalina's as if they were looking for something. They must be waiting to waylay my brother or anyone he sends on his behalf."

When we got to the Pereiras' home, we saw a horse hitched to a tree in the courtyard, and Father said, "That must be his horse."

We went inside and Melchor, my father's friend, took us to an inner room. "Here is the man who came to see you, Rodrigo," he said.

"I bring a message from your brother," the stranger said and took a scroll tied with a thin string from the folds of his tunic.

Father removed the string quickly and unrolled the

scroll. He read, and I saw the relief on his face.

I reached out my hand and father put the scroll in it. I read it, but didn't understand what I was reading. The words written on it looked very strange to me.

"Did you just come from Cádiz?" my father asked the stranger, who nodded.

I'd heard about Cádiz, which was a fairly large city on the Mediterranean Sea near the Portuguese border.

"And will you be going back there tonight?" my father asked.

"Yes, sir. Don Alonso needs the money urgently."

"Wait for me here. I'll be right back."

I stayed with the messenger in Melchor's house and was surprised to see him change right in front of my eyes. At first he'd looked like an old man because he was stooped, and he had a white mustache and a turban covering part of his face. Now, he straightened up, took off the turban, and pulled off the mustache that had been pasted on under his nose.

I looked at him with my mouth open, and he smiled at me and said, "You can see, my boy, that it's no easy job to be a secret messenger."

"But why did you have to disguise yourself?" I asked.

"If someone saw me come, he will now see someone else leave."

"And the horse?"

"You are a clever boy," the man said, smiling. "Look," he said and spread a piece of green cloth on the floor at my feet. "My horse wears a disguise too."

Chapter Four
SUKKOT IN THE FIELDS

Father returned to the Pereiras' home with Aunt Catalina, who questioned the messenger about her husband. "Where is he? When did you see him last? Does he look well? How does he live?" She asked him other questions too, but most of them were left unanswered

"Whatever your husband wanted to tell you is written in the message," the stranger said.

After scribbling some letters on a piece of paper, my aunt reread the scroll, translating the secret code that she and my father understood: "B ptl yhkmngtmx xghnza mh ybgw t ltyx atkuhk" became "I was fortunate enough to find a safe harbor."

"Ixhiex bg lxobeex tkx ybgwbgz hnm yhk fx patm max mxlmbfhgr tztbglm fx ptl" translated as "People in Seville are finding out for me what the testimony against me was."

Later, father explained the code. "You write the alphabet on a piece of paper. Then you write the alphabet again, right above it. But this time you begin with the letter H. We used H because Hashem is another name for our God. Then you substitute the letter in the top line for the letter in the bottom line."

My aunt showed me the two rows of letters she had written down in order translate the message:

H I J K L M N O P Q R S T U V W X Y Z A B C D E F G

A B C D E F G H I J K L M N O P Q R S T U V W X Y Z

Father made me figure out how to write my name in the code. M had a T right above it and A had an H. I finally managed to write down "thubls." It wasn't much of a name and we all laughed. But then Father became serious. "Never forget this code, Manuel. We might need it some day too."

At midnight, the messenger left for Cádiz, and we—my Aunt Catalina, my father, and I—spent the night at Melchor's house. We were afraid that walking around outside at night might arouse suspicion.

"I am so relieved," I heard my father say to my aunt. "They won't catch up to Alonso before we find out what the accusations against him are. It won't be easy, but I know our family will spare no expense in finding someone with connections to the Inquisition Court who will sell us the information. Once we know the accusations, we will hire the best defense lawyer. What do you think your servant could have said to the authorities?"

"He worked for us two years ago, and only for a short time. I hardly remember him. Alonso caught him lying and sent him away immediately."

"If that is true, what could he say about you?" Father asked.

"We're very careful, Rodrigo. Even the servants who have been working in our house for years could not say very much about us," my aunt replied.

"Do you remember what time of year he worked for you?"

"Why are you asking, Rodrigo?"

"It's important to know whether he was there during one of the fasts!"

"That isn't relevant, Rodrigo. Even during the Great Fast and on the Queen Esther Fast we fill the kitchen with food to mislead the servants."

Aunt Catalina went on talking, but I stopped listening to their conversation. I was thinking about how lucky we were to have relatives. All of them left Portugal before us. Uncle Alonso's family came to Spain first, and he is now a rich man. His workers dye cloth in the shed next to his house, and then he sells the dyed cloth in his shop. The house we live in belongs to him. I think he bought it especially for us when we came to Spain. Right from the beginning, he wanted us to come to Seville, but my father wanted to try his luck in the big city first. He hoped he would get a position as a doctor in the king's court. In Portugal, my father was well known as an excellent doctor, and his reputation reached as far as Madrid. But he couldn't get a *limpieza* certificate showing he had been a Christian for a long time and that kept him from getting the position. I wasn't sorry. I was glad to leave Madrid and move close to my aunts and uncles.

We'd come to Seville without a penny. My father couldn't find work in Madrid, and the money we brought with us from Portugal wasn't even enough for a year. Almost everything we have, we got from our aunts and uncles. At the beginning, they gave us money too. Now, Father is starting to make a good living, and we can buy things for ourselves.

They gave us a very warm welcome here. Aunt Tereza, who is Mother's sister, filled our kitchen with delicious food. She makes such wonderful dishes: spicy fish with rice, which I love; peppery soups; and bean and lentil stew. And Aunt Tereza makes delicious sweets: grape and fig jam cakes filled with dates, cinnamon cookies, semolina cake, and so much more.

Tereza's husband, my Uncle Lorenzo, wasn't in Seville at the time. He was another wealthy uncle—a spice merchant in Spain and other countries. The Monsanto family, that is, my Aunt Tereza and her husband, had two sons: Federico and Diego. Federico, the older one, was studying at the Alcalá de Henares University in Castile. The younger son, Diego, helped his father in the business. When Lorenzo was out of the city, Diego came to our house to teach me Latin, arithmetic, and geometry. And he taught me literature too.

I couldn't fall asleep the night I stayed with my father and Aunt Catalina in the Pereiras' house. I tossed and turned on the mattress and tried to think of nice things—so that if I did manage to fall asleep, I'd have pleasant dreams.

I thought about the holiday we'd have next week. It was the holiday that Aunt Tereza and Remedios had made all that good food for.

Father told me that it was a holiday we celebrate out in the fields, far from the city, so nobody would see us. "We'll be in *sukkot*, huts like the ones vineyard guards put up, and we'll stay in them for a few days," Father said and explained that the Torah of Moses commands us to remember the *sukkot* our forefathers lived in when they came out of Egypt. Father told me that Moses, or Moshe, was a prophet who received the commandments straight from God.

Last year at this time, we were in Madrid, and we couldn't obey the *mitzvah*, or commandment, to stay in a *sukkah*. Even in Bragança, I don't remember spending a few days in a *sukkah*.

But here we could leave the city for a few days without making people suspicious. Mother had already told our maid, Ana, that she would have a vacation because the family was traveling to a wedding in Córdoba. Aunt Catalina and Aunt Tereza told their maids the same thing.

Father ordered two wagons for the following week, and I asked him to let me drive one. But he said that my cousins Fernando and Diego, who were older and more experienced than I was, would drive the wagons.

We'd load the food and our belongings onto one wagon and ride in the other one. It would be a little crowded. We were five, Aunt Catalina would come with Fernando and Mencia, who's a year younger than I am, and Aunt Tereza would come with Diego. Altogether, we'd be squeezing ten people into the wagon!

Fernando told me about the fields where we'd spend the Sukkot holiday. "The fields are behind hills and you can't see them from the road. The horses pulling the wagons have to work very hard to get there," Fernando said. "But after that, they can rest for a long time because we'll stay in the same place until it's time to go back."

I wonder what we'll do in the sukkah, I thought. Maybe Father will tell us about the Torah of Moses—that'll be very interesting. Then I remembered that he couldn't tell us anything about our religion because of Juan. My little brother thought he was Christian, and it would take a few years for him to be old enough to hear the truth.

Oh, Juan will be happy in the field, I said to myself. He can run around as much as he wants just as long as he doesn't ask me to play with him. Sometimes he pesters me about that, until I have to yell at him to stop.

I did manage to fall asleep for a while. I know that because of a dream I had that night. In my dream, I'm in a large green *sukkah* with my cousin Fernando—who naturally knows about our real religion too—and we're talking about Moses, who took our forefathers out of Egypt because they were slaves there. And suddenly, Juan starts running around us. I yell at him to go out and play in the fields, and then the *guardas* appear. "We've come to take you." I jump up and shout, "We didn't do anything!" And I managed to hear one of them say, "Tell that to the Inquisitor," before my father woke me up.

Father shook me and whispered for me to be quiet. "Hush, Manuel, or you'll wake up everyone."

I told him that I had a scary dream. In the morning, when I told him about it, he said, "You must be excited about the holiday. Try not to think about it."

But when I told my sister about the dream, she turned pale and said, "I hope it isn't an omen that bad things will happen. I'm very scared, and I've already asked Mother if it wouldn't be better to cancel the trip."

"Don't you dare say anything like that, Remedios!" I burst out. "We've never celebrated this holiday, and I really want to go out to the fields and live in a *sukkah*."

"I see that you're still a little boy," my sister rebuked me. "All you want are adventures. Don't you realize how dangerous it is? Especially now, when everyone suspects us because of Alonso!"

I didn't say anything. My sister's words hit home. I suppose I was acting like a child in a way. But even so, I kept hoping we'd be able to have our adventure in the fields.

My cousin Diego came to teach me arithmetic, and that distracted me from *Sukkot*. I solved a few problems using the method Diego showed me, and then he asked me about the night before.

I told him what had happened in Melchor Pereira's house, and I described the disguised messenger.

"That man," Diego said, "took his life in his hands. If they'd caught him with the letter on him, they would have tortured him until he told them where Alonso was hiding, and they would have punished him severely for helping *conversos*."

"But the message was written in code," I cried.

"The Inquisitors can decipher that code. They have ways of doing that."

"What ways?"

"They would have arrested the person the letter was

addressed to, in this case, your father, and they would have laid him out on the torture rack until he blurted out the answer to their question. Now, let's go back to our arithmetic problems," Diego said.

"I was up all night, Diego. We didn't get back from Melchor Pereira's house until this morning, and I'm very tired. Maybe you can teach me next week, when we go out to the fields?" I asked.

"It's not definite that we're going this time. A member of the family disappeared, and that makes us all suspicious in the eyes of the *Santo Oficio*. That's what I heard your father say to my mother this morning," Diego said and sighed.

"What did Aunt Tereza answer?"

"She said that it's up to your Aunt Catalina," Diego replied.

Diego went home at noon and we got ready for the Sabbath. We bathed and put on clean clothes—being careful to hide them under our old clothes, so that no one would be suspicious of us. Juan was the only one in the family who didn't change clothes, and he was sent to the market with Ana. We added new wicks to the oil candles, and at four-thirty, Mother lit them.

There was a pleasant aroma in the air because of the mint and other fragrant leaves we put in water.

Father poured wine into a glass and said, "Blessed art Thou oh Lord our God, Creator of the fruit of the vine." He drank and gave the glass to Mother. My sister and I drank from it too.

Then Father put one hand on Remedios's head and the other on mine, and blessed us, asking God to watch over us.

We dipped our hands in water and Father just had time to complete the Hebrew blessing over the bread before Ana and Juan came back from the market. After the meal, we all went to Aunt Catalina's house. I saw my father whispering with my aunt, and I moved closer to hear what they were saying. I knew it had something to do with *Sukkot*.

Father said, "We'll pay for the horses and wagons, but we won't go."

Before I had time to feel bad, Aunt Catalina said, "No. We'll do what we do every year. If we carry out the commandments of the Torah of our forefathers, that will help Alonso and save us from the danger that threatens us."

Chapter Five
THE OUTBREAK OF AN EPIDEMIC?

Ana had Saturday off and she could go home to her village. Before she left, Mother asked her to turn on the stove so the food could cook.

My Aunt Catalina had told my mother to do that, so everyone could see smoke coming from our chimney and they wouldn't suspect us of not lighting fire on the Sabbath.

Mother took the spindle and sat down at the window without touching it. But the neighbors and the watchers couldn't know that she wasn't really working.

Father went out to see his patients, and this time he let Juan go with him. Why? So that my little brother could take the money instead of Father. Juan was proud to have that job and boasted about the doubloons in the leather pouch he was holding as if they were his.

Our relatives came to have lunch with us, and together, we planned our wagon trip to the fields far from the city. We had one more day to plan, Sunday, because the eve of *Sukkot* fell on Monday. We knew the exact day from the Hebrew calendar Melchor had received from his uncle in Bordeaux.

On Sunday, Mother gave Juan clean clothes, and we all went to church.

At the entrance to the church, we lifted our hands as if we were going to cross ourselves, and then we lowered them slowly. We went to our seats and waited for Padre Versano to come in. He was our priest, the man my parents confessed to.

When he gave me a piece of the holy bread, I put it under my tongue like my father taught me, but I spit out as much of it as I could later.

Padre Versano gave a sermon about the evil Jews who taunted Jesus and caused him to be crucified. He held a huge cross in his hands, and when prayers were over, we had to file past it and kiss it. I looked to see what my father did. He brought his lips close to the cross, but I don't think they touched it.

I knew that the cross was unclean for me, and I was afraid I'd get so close that my lips would touch it. I decided to try and get out of it—to walk past quickly and kiss the air. But when I looked at my father's face and saw the expression in his eyes, I understood that I shouldn't put us in danger. I felt nauseous. Something inside me turned hard as iron. My neck tensed and I was afraid I wouldn't be able to bend it even if I wanted to.

I closed my eyes so I didn't have to see and felt my lips burn when they touched the cross. I kept walking slowly in the line. Only my heart was racing madly in my chest.

On the way home, I thought about the fact that not too long ago, I used to kiss the cross without even thinking about it. I was surprised that I'd changed so much that I almost couldn't go near it now.

When Diego came, I told him how I'd felt in church, and he said that it was the same with him. And he had an explanation. "Before we knew the truth, we crossed ourselves and kissed the cross without thinking about it. But we still felt that we were different, and it bothered us. They call us *cristianos nuevos* even though the Jewish converts to Christianity have been acting like good Christians, at least on the outside, for almost two hundred years.

"Even though you didn't know that you were Jewish, Manuel, you felt it in your heart. So actually, you haven't changed in any real way."

"But . . ." I started to say, and stopped when I saw Juan come into the room.

"Diego, when are you going to start teaching me arithmetic?" my brother asked.

"You'll learn it from your brother, Juanito. Manuel will teach you arithmetic." My brother didn't like my cousin's answer, and he made a face. He was probably trying to think of a good answer (I could see that from his expression). But he saw something that distracted him. The candles we'd lit on the Sabbath eve were still burning, and he ran over to them.

"No," I cried. But Diego signaled me to be quiet.

"It's a waste of oil," my little brother said. "Everyone's always telling me to put out candles when there's light."

I couldn't tell him that they were holy candles, Sabbath candles, and we weren't supposed to put them out.

He looked at me, waiting for an explanation, and I turned to Diego for help.

"Come here, Juanito," my cousin said, answering my silent plea. "Let's see what you know about simple arithmetic. You know how to add and subtract?"

"And I know how to multiply numbers," Juan said. "If you multiply two by three, you get six, right?"

Diego praised my brother and wrote down some problems for him to solve by himself and leave us to our business. But now that Juan was with us, we couldn't go on talking about what we had before, so we started working on geometry.

Mother and Remedios were busy getting ready for the next day: packing dishes, household items, and clothes; putting food into boxes; and baking cakes.

Father was preparing medicines to take with us, and in the middle, two boys from Alfonso de Castro's family came to call him to their father's bed. "Father is burning up with fever," they said, "and his whole body is shaking."

I stayed to watch over the medicines that were cooking in the kitchen, and Father went out to see Don de Castro, who owned large vineyards and was an important man in Seville. When he came back, the medicines were ready.

Father had only been home for about an hour when someone came to call him again. This time it was a little girl who'd gotten sick and her father was very worried. "The pain is so bad that Cordelia is weeping. She says that her head is splitting from the inside."

Father went with the man to treat his daughter, and

when he came back, he found Diego waiting for him so they could go to get the wagons. We loaded them with everything we'd prepared for the trip. Before sunrise, we went to pick up Aunt Catalina, my cousin Mencia, and Fernando. Diego brought his mother, Aunt Tereza, and early in the morning, before people were up and about in the streets, we were already outside of Seville.

I sat between Fernando and Juan in the wagon, and Mencia sat across from me. We were all squeezed in between the bundles and the boxes that filled the wagon, but we were in high spirits.

We were quiet, waiting expectantly for what would come, and every once in a while we would smile and sigh happily. As long as we were traveling on the main road to Málaga, the ride was pleasant enough, although we were very crowded in the wagon. But after about two hours, when we left the road and rode through the fields between the hills, we were jostled so hard that I felt as if parts of my body were splitting off into separate pieces. Sometimes the wagon banged us around so much that I was sure we were going to fly out over the field. We bounced and fell over each other and onto the bundles and boxes that got all jumbled together. A box that had pickled olives and all kinds of squash in it turned upside down and opened, and the squash was smashed and the olives rolled all over the floor of the wagon.

Juan squealed with happiness. He enjoyed bouncing up into the air and landing—and it didn't matter who or what he landed on. We were all happy. Only Aunt Catalina had a tense, serious look on her face.

"Did we take a wrong turn?" my mother asked Diego, who was driving the horses. We stopped and Fernando, who was driving the other wagon, stopped his horses too.

Aunt Catalina looked around and then cried out to her son, "Fernando, Ines is asking if this is the way. Maybe we made a mistake?"

"No, Mother, I remember exactly where those hills are. And there's another sign—that mountain over there that's shaped like a person's face."

We all looked in the direction Fernando was pointing to, and we really did see a mountain that looked like the face of a gigantic statue.

"*Yahee*," Diego spurred his horses to start moving, and we held tightly onto the boards of the wagon as it jerked up the hills over stones and thorny bushes.

"I hope the wheels don't break," Father said, leaning over the railing of the wagon, and he almost fell off when it flew over a deep pit.

Fernando was right. Behind the hills—hidden by them—was the field where the family always built its *sukkah*. Actually, the basic structure of the *sukkah* was already there from earlier years, and all we had to do was attach the strips of cloth Catalina had brought from their shop to the bare posts, and then lay branches across the strips to make a leafy roof.

Diego, Fernando, Juan, and I went to bring branches from the trees growing on the hills. Father tied the pieces of cloth to the poles, and the women organized everything we'd brought with us.

Juan dragged behind him the branches that Diego

had taken off the trees, and when he got to the *sukkah*, he shouted, "I'm hungry! I'm hungry!"

Aunt Tereza had already put a pot on the fire that Father had built between two stones, and the smell of fish spread through the valley.

We went to dip our hands in the spring. Father whispered the blessing over the bread and we all attacked the good food waiting for us on the mat inside the *sukkah*.

While we were eating, I suddenly heard the sound of crying and was surprised to see who it was coming from.

Aunt Catalina couldn't stop weeping, and Mother put her arm around her shoulder. Through her tears, she said, "Alonso dear, where are you?"

"But you know that he's in a safe place," my father said to her in a firm voice.

"A safe place," my aunt repeated and shook her head hopelessly. "You know as well as I do how long the arms of the *Santo Oficio* are, and the city of Cádiz is probably no different from ours, full of watchers and spies."

"I trust my brother not to be staying in the city. He must have found refuge in a remote village in the area!"

"Strangers stick out more in small places. Oh, Rodrigo, I'm so worried about my husband."

"We are all worried," my mother said, and hugged Aunt Catalina. "We'll pray to God that we see Alonso soon, and everything will go back to being the way it was!"

Night fell, and the silence was occasionally broken

by the shrieks of night birds. I lay on my mat in the *sukkah* and looked at the stars showing through the branches of the roof.

I said to myself: If only there was a shooting star. Then I could make a wish that Uncle Alonso would be able to come back to Seville. If only it turns out that his servant's testimony to the Inquisition cannot not prove anything against him. And then I decided to think about happy things so I would have good dreams.

What would we do tomorrow? Climb the hills. Take walks. Play catch-me-if-you-can. Juan says he runs faster than I can. Ha-ha, tomorrow I'll show him . . .

I must have fallen asleep, because I really did dream about running, but not in a game. I dreamed I caught up to Juan and told him to come quickly because a squadron of *guardas* was chasing us. I was very scared, so scared that I woke up and was happy to find myself next to my father in the *sukkah*.

The next day, when we were eating breakfast in the *sukkah*, I saw the worry lines on Father's forehead. My mother also saw that Father was worried and she said, "You look ill today, Rodrigo. Don't you feel well?"

"I didn't sleep last night," Father said. "I'm very worried."

"Aren't we all worried? But even so, I think we all slept so deeply that none of us noticed the rain that fell during the night," Mother said and smiled.

"I noticed it. But it was a drizzle. I couldn't fall asleep because I was thinking about whether there isn't a connection between what I saw in the home of my sick patient, Alfonso de Castro, and the illness of the

girl I examined on Sunday evening." He took a deep breath and blew it out through his lips.

"What connection could there be?"

"The symptoms I saw could turn out to be nothing, but they could prove to be..." My father stopped speaking.

"Be what, Rodrigo?" My mother demanded a reply.

"Let me be, Ines. What is the point of talking about things that may have no truth at all!"

"We have the right to know why you are worried."

"They say," my father replied slowly, "they say that an epidemic has broken out in Bragança."

"An epidemic?" the women cried out in panic.

"An epidemic of what, Rodrigo?" mother asked.

"The plague. The black plague."

"And you think the plague has reached Seville?" Aunt Catalina asked.

"It could have," Father said, shaking his head and adding, "Why didn't I think of it sooner? My mind must have been completely occupied with this trip," he said, shaking his head again, as if in sorrow or despair.

"What is this plague you're talking about?" Juan asked. "What's a plague epidemic?"

After Diego explained it to him, my little brother said to Father, "Everyone must be looking for you now. You're the only one who can help the people who have the disease."

"There is not much that can be done for it," Father told Juan and sighed.

For the next two hours, we watched Father walk around the hills, and it looked to me as if he were walking in circles. I wanted to go to him and ask what the symptoms of the plague were, and I had other questions too, but I sensed that he wanted to be alone.

I remembered the games I'd planned for today, but I didn't have the slightest desire to play. I didn't mention them to Fernando or Juan.

The women were busy making lunch and talking, but I couldn't hear them. I went to the spring, drank its cold water, and looked at the small creatures in it. Suddenly, I saw my father's face reflected in it. I looked up and saw him standing next to me.

"I am thinking of returning to Seville," he said, "I am sure your mother will understand."

I was very proud that my father was sharing his thoughts with me and telling me about them before he told the others. "It's all right, Father," I told him. "We'll manage here and there won't be any problems. But how will you get back?"

"I'll take one of the wagons and return as soon as I can."

When Father told Mother that he was planning to return, I heard her say, "But maybe there is no epidemic, and you're going back for no reason!"

"His duty calls him, Ines, and he will have no rest until he goes to see what is happening in Seville," Aunt Catalina said, interrupting their conversation.

And Father got up and left on his journey.

Chapter Six
NIGHT PROCESSIONS

Every morning, we went high into the hills to look out into the distance—maybe we'd see Father's wagon. And when one day, at noon, we saw it—before it disappeared behind a hill—we shouted happily. We waited to see it again, and then we ran to tell everyone the news.

Father didn't have to say anything. We read it all on his face. But we'd known even before then that an epidemic had broken out because he hadn't come back the next day.

A few days before, Father had looked like a man in his prime, and now—when he came back from Seville— he looked as if he'd shrunk. His body was thin and his face pale and gaunt.

"What are all those bundles on the wagon?" Mother asked. "After all, we're going back today!"

Father shook his head.

"We're not going back?" Aunt Catalina and my mother asked together.

"We were fortunate to leave Seville when we did," Father said, still shaking his head. "The black plague is destroying the city. People are dying so fast that they can't be buried . . ."

"Have any of our relatives, our friends, died?" Mother asked, horrified.

"Alfonso de Castro, who owns the vineyards, his wife, and three of their four children. Melchor Pereira's son and two of the family's servants. And that girl I was called to see on Sunday, Cordelia, died, along with her father and her brother. And many more, too many to count.

"The epidemic has struck especially hard at the quarter where the Moors live."

"Aldino!" I cried. "Did you see my friend Aldino, the son of the *borceguinero* who repaired Mother's sandals?"

Father was in no hurry to answer me. He looked at me as he considered what to say, and I felt my skin break out in goose bumps.

Father turned his head and sighed. "He's not dead. I saw him and he looked strong and healthy."

I sensed that Father wasn't telling me the whole truth, and I also felt that he didn't have the heart to talk to us.

I heard my Aunt Tereza say, "Rodrigo is exhausted." And before she finished saying the words, Father's eyes closed. His head fell onto his chest and he fell asleep sitting up.

I couldn't speak to Father from noon until the next morning because he slept the whole time and we were careful not to wake him up. Even Juan spoke in a whisper. The things father told us had a strong effect on us, and we were worried that he might have caught that terrible disease.

Father had always told us that if we don't want to get sick, we have to sleep well, eat three meals a day, and keep our bodies clean. From the way Father looked when he came back from Seville, we could tell that he hadn't followed even one of those rules.

I heard Mother say to Aunt Tereza, "I don't think Rodrigo went home at all. He must have rushed around from one sick person's house to another the whole time."

The next morning, I got up early and went out for a walk. When I got back, Mother and Aunt Catalina were standing in the *sukkah* looking at my still-sleeping Father.

"Look at him, skin and bones," Mother murmured.

"If he rests for a few days and eats Tereza's food, he'll get his strength back," my aunt whispered.

"Come Catalina, let's go outside so we don't wake him up."

After they went out, I saw Father get up and I ran over to him. "Were you at Aldino's house, Father?"

He didn't answer me right away. He stretched. He yawned. Then he looked at me with red eyes. "What did you ask me, Manuel?"

"I asked about Aldino."

"Yes, I saw him. Poor boy, his parents and his younger brothers died. Only he and his older brother have remained alive."

"Who'll take care of them, Father? How will they live?"

Father shrugged and sighed.

"We have to help them now that they're orphans. And Aldino is a good boy. He's my friend!"

"There is someone who will take care of him, Manuel," Father said and looked down.

"Who?"

"Oh, Rodrigo, you finally woke up," Mother said from the entrance to the *sukkah*. "I was afraid you were ill."

"I am as healthy as a bull, Ines dear," Father said with a smile, and sniffed the air. "The aroma of fresh bread. I'll go to wash in the spring and come back to eat. I suddenly feel very hungry."

"If you're hungry, that's a sign that you're healthy," Mother said with a sigh of relief.

I wanted to go with him so he could tell me who was taking care of Aldino, but my cousin Mencia came in carrying a small loaf of hot bread.

"Here, Manuel, I kneaded the dough and baked it myself," she said, handing me the bread, which was the size of an apple, "It's good."

I knew that I was supposed to dip my hands in water and say a blessing before eating. But Mencia still didn't know the secret of our religion, so I acted the way Father told me I should when strangers were around—I thanked her and ate the bread. And it really was delicious.

Father came back and we sat down to eat. He said, "You should all stay here. That way, you will not be in danger of catching the disease."

"But what about . . ." Aunt Catalina began to object.

Father didn't let her go on. "Alonso has most certainly heard about what is happening in Seville, and he would not endanger himself by coming at such a time. He hasn't sent messengers either. I know my brother well. He will wait where he is in hiding until he knows exactly what the situation is."

"But the epidemic may have spread to Cádiz and . . ." My Aunt did not finish her sentence. Mencia's sobbing interrupted her.

My sister, Remedios, went and sat down next to Mencia. I heard her whisper something to our cousin, and I was curious to know what it was. But my curiosity passed when Father continued speaking.

"There are some things that man can control, and there are some things that are in God's hands. What we can do now is try not to catch the disease. We'll stay here and be saved. As for Alonso, we'll pray that God is with him, and I'm sure our prayers will be answered."

"Let's pray now," Mencia cried. "Maybe if we all pray together, God will hear. Oh, Holy Mother, Father and the Holy Ghost; Oh Jesus our gracious Savior . . ." Mencia prayed, her clear voice ringing out, and none of us joined in. Puzzled, she looked at us until Remedios whispered something in her ear and she nodded as if she understood.

"What will they think if we don't go back?" Aunt Catalina asked. "And the wagon owner—won't he demand his wagons back?"

"The owner of the wagons is dead. I saw his wife and paid her what she asked. But I'm not sure that she will live to enjoy the money. She had a high fever and severe chills."

"And what about the servants?" Aunt Tereza asked. "They must be waiting for us!"

"Naturally, I went to your house several times, and it was closed up. The servants have most likely stayed in their villages, if they're still alive. And the same is true for your house, Catalina—there was no one there and no one will be concerned about where you are if you do not return on time."

"And you, Rodrigo, you will stay here with us!" my mother said as if it were clear he would.

Father waved his hand to indicate *no*. "I am going back to Seville today."

"But Father, you said there wasn't very much to do against that disease!" I reminded him what he had said before he went back to Seville.

"I can ease the suffering, Manuel. There are medicines that help. But mainly, I have to prevent the spread of the epidemic. I am in charge of getting rid of the rats, and I oversee the burial of the dead. I make sure the city is clean, and I help with whatever I can."

"There are other doctors in Seville besides you, Rodrigo. And you're new in that city. . ." Mother pointed out.

Father stopped her before she could go on. "What I saw in the Moorish quarter was very sad. It was on the last night I was there. The dead were piled up in the streets and grief-stricken people carrying torches walked among them, beating themselves with sticks and scratching their flesh with thorns. They walked and wept—men, women, and children. There were two of us trying to help the sick. We went into their dilapidated shacks and were shocked at the crowded conditions and the filth inside them. It's no wonder that the epidemic spread so quickly in that quarter.

"I saw a familiar face in one of the shacks. It was Aldino, and I hardly recognized him. His eyes were swollen from crying. He and his brother were kneeling beside their dead parents and brothers, and they refused to leave.

"Suddenly, a group of monks burst into the shack singing something from the Gospels, and as they sang, they grabbed the two boys by the hands and took them with them. Where to? I don't know. I followed them out and saw the monks join the procession. But I wasn't able to see what they did with Aldino and his brother because it was dark. Maybe the boys stayed with them in the procession, and maybe they were taken someplace else.

"At least Aldino and brother were taken from the infected house, and that may have saved their lives!"

Chapter Seven
ALONSO RETURNS

Father came in a wagon to take us back to Seville, and Uncle Lorenzo, Aunt Tereza's husband, back from his business trips, was with him. They brought us all gifts. Mencia got a porcelain doll, and I got a knife inset with a precious purple stone.

It's funny, I thought, how much that doll looked like Mencia. They both had clear white skin, a small red mouth, and pink cheeks. And I found another similarity between them: They both had sad eyes.

Once, Mencia had been a laughing, mischievous little girl, and now, after her father had disappeared, she almost never laughed. I saw her hold the doll close to her heart and heard her whisper, "If only you could pray to the Holy Mother for us."

When would they finally tell her? After all, she isn't a little girl who can't understand and who might give the secret away thoughtlessly!

I asked my sister what she said to Mencia when she wanted us all to pray to Jesus together, and Remedios replied, "I told her that it wasn't nice that a little girl should decide when it was time to pray, and I promised her that we'd all pray in church soon."

"Don't you think it's time to tell her the truth?"

"It's not up to us. Her parents are probably waiting until she's twelve. That's how old I was when they told me. Grandfather told me. Almost everything I know about our religion, I learned from him. And he told me such wonderful stories—about how our forefathers came out of Egypt after God inflicted the Egyptians with ten plagues; about King Solomon, the wisest of all men, who knew how to speak to animals; about Queen Esther..."

"Remedios," I interrupted her when I remembered the secrecy that surrounded Grandfather's death, the questions I'd asked then that were never really answered, "What did Grandfather die of?"

"His brother, Felipe, was being held in the Inquisition cellars in Lisbon. The Inquisitors tried to get him to confess that he believed in the Torah of Moses and denied that Jesus was the messiah. If he confessed, they would arrest the entire family—including Grandfather's family—which means us. The Inquisition knew that if one person in a family practiced the religion of his forefathers, then the other members of the family did too."

"But what did Grandfather die of?" I cried impatiently.

My sister looked at me sadly, breathing heavily as if I'd made her angry, and whispered, "When they came from the Inquisition to tell Grandfather that Felipe had died during the interrogation, he dropped like a stone onto the ground. Our father couldn't reach him in time, and he died. Grandfather knew the kind of tortures his elderly brother had gone through," Remedios said. When I saw her brown eyes fill with tears, I was sorry that I'd reminded her by asking.

I looked for something to say that would make her think about other things. "Remedios, did you hear what Father said about the *regidores* in Seville, how hard they're trying—along with the monks—to help the people who have the plague?"

My sister nodded and said, "Yes, it's very good that they set up a special hospital. And father said that the monks are helping everywhere."

When we got back to Seville, there weren't many victims of the black plague left, and they were all together in the special hospital set up by the church people together with the city councilmen. It was good to be home after being away for such a long time. During the last part of our stay, we froze from the cold in the *sukkah*, and our house seemed like a palace.

The first few days back in Seville, they didn't let me or Juan go out into the street. They were still afraid of the plague. I sat at the window and looked out at the alley. But there wasn't much to see, because there were so few people. The city had emptied out because of the plague. It was interesting that fewer *conversos* had gotten the disease. True, some had died: the son of Melchor Pereira, father's friend; three members of the Gomez family; and some others who I didn't know. But in the Christian families, thousands had died.

Remedios told me that it was no accident that we, the *conversos*, had suffered less from the disease. She said it was to show the pure Christians that we were the ones God loved.

I asked Mother what she thought about that, and she said, "What Remedios says is true. Because God loves us, He gave us commandments to follow that protect us."

"I don't understand."

"Manuel, think about what your father told us about hygiene, about keeping clean especially when we're in danger of catching a disease. And our religion commands us to wash our hands before every meal and . . ."

Mother stopped because Juan came in. When would my little brother finally grow up so that we could trust him to keep our secret?

That morning, I saw our neighbor's daughter, Violanti, who was about my age, standing at the window of the apartment on the other side of the narrow alley. She didn't turn away from the window when she saw me. I was surprised, because it wasn't nice for girls to act like that. I saw that she was staying where she was, so I called to her, "*Buenos días*," and she replied, "Are you back already?"

That seemed like a pretty stupid question to me as I was obviously back, but I figured that she only said it to start a conversation, so I nodded.

"Where were you?" she asked.

Father taught me not to trust anyone; you can never know where a trap is hidden. I gave her the same answer we gave to everyone: "We were visiting relatives in Córdoba."

"What did you do there?"

What a nosy girl, I said to myself, but I answered her because I did not want to appear rude.

"Someone in our family got married there, in Córdoba."

Violanti laughed and said, "That was a very long wedding!"

I didn't answer and I felt like ending the conversation, when she said, "Wait, don't go. I'm home alone and if I don't talk to you, I'll start to get scared again, like I was before I saw you at the window."

"Where are your parents?"

Violanti shrugged to say she didn't know.

I thought she was acting strangely. I didn't know her well, and in fact that was the first time I'd ever spoken to her. I knew her name and she knew mine because she'd been in our house twice with her mother.

"Why were you scared?"

Violanti shrugged her shoulders again.

A strange girl, I said to myself.

"But Manuel, your father stayed here in the city. Why didn't he go to that wedding?"

"He came back to Seville because of the epidemic."

"Yes, he helped everyone. They say he's the best doctor in Seville and Jesus sent him here especially so he could help save the people who deserved to be saved."

"Is that what they say?"

"They say that the epidemic broke out because the people in Seville did bad things and weren't good Christians. That's why so many were punished and died. But the plague is blind and can't tell the differ-

64

ence between the guilty and the innocent. That's why Jesus sent your father here, to save the good people. You mean you didn't know that?"

"I haven't had time to talk to anyone yet. You're the first person I've talked to since we came back to Seville."

"How old are you, Manuel?"

"I'll be twelve soon. How old are you?"

"I'm twelve and a half already," Violanti boasted.

Again, I felt like walking away from the window.

"Manuel," Violanti called, probably guessing what I was thinking, "Could you come to my house? My throat hurts from yelling from window to window like this."

"To your house?!" I didn't believe what I was hearing. Since when did boys go to the houses of girls (especially older girls, like her) who aren't part of the family?

"Please, Manuel, I can't stay alone in the house anymore!"

"I'll ask my sister if she wants to go," I said and went into the kitchen to see if my sister was there. Ana, our maid, hadn't come back to us yet, and Remedios helped Mother prepare meals. I heard Violanti's voice shouting behind me, "Never mind, Manuel, never mind," but I ignored it.

Remedios raised her eyebrows in puzzlement when I told her what Violanti wanted.

"She must be very frightened," Remedios said and went to the window with me.

"Would you like me to come over to keep you company, Violanti?" Remedios asked.

"I think my parents will be back soon," Violanti replied, "and I'll lie down to rest till then."

My sister and I looked at each other, and when we did, Violanti went back into the room and we didn't see her anymore.

"A strange girl," my sister said as she returned to the kitchen, and I nodded in agreement.

I was glad when Diego finally arrived to teach me Latin, because I was pretty bored.

"I'll leave you some books and you can do some studying on your own," Diego said. "Now that my father's back from Córdoba, I have to work with him, and tomorrow we're going to Madrid on business."

I had mixed feelings about what my cousin said. More than I liked studying, I liked sitting and talking with Diego. Now I'd have a break from studying—because I wasn't planning to do it on my own—but I'd miss Diego's company. Who could I talk to the way I talked to him?

Fernando, who was my best friend, had gotten closemouthed. Remedios was busy, and Juan was too young. I could go to Aunt Catalina's house and be with Mencia. But I realized that even though I liked her, it was too hard to be with someone who didn't know our secret. And I thought again that it was too bad they didn't tell Mencia.

On Sunday, the whole family went to church. It was half empty. Our priest had died of the plague, and there was a new one in his place, Padre Pedro. I saw Violanti and her parents, who looked pretty old, in the row in front of us. Mother told me that Violanti had older brothers and sisters, all married, and she was the child of their old age.

No one in the church moved when Padre Pedro talked about the victims of the epidemic. He said, "Good people sacrificed themselves for others who have sinned and brought this terrible epidemic to our city. But they will not be cleansed of their sins. Only those who confess their evil deeds and ask for forgiveness can purify themselves and cleanse our city of the contagion that has infected it.

"The Jews sold our messiah and sinned against the whole world. They are the source of the evil. You probably thought that all of that belongs to the past, but that is not so. Today too, there are those who mock the image of our messiah and bring disaster down upon our heads. But we will uproot them from our midst, we will not rest until we find them.

"Anyone who can tell us of such a criminal will be blessed by our saints, who seek our welfare, the welfare of humanity. It is the duty of each one of us to find and expose the evil before we are inflicted with additional calamities. If any one of you knows hypocrites or people who come to the holy church and pretend to pray to our saints and then spit—if not with their mouths, then with their hearts—on the image of our messiah, it is your sacred duty to speak up. Anyone who hides testimony of such importance from our holy institution will be cursed by the church, and even if he takes the sacraments, he will lose his place in the next world. For that man's criminal silence makes him a partner of the heretics, and he will burn in the fires of hell along with them.

"The man or woman who gives testimony about others, or about themselves, will be forgiven their trespasses. And after they give their testimony, their souls will rest in peace. Their days will pass pleasantly, and they will sleep at night like babes."

My heart pounded with fear as I listened to Padre Pedro's sermon, and I didn't dare raise my eyes to look at anyone, not even my parents.

At first, when we went into the church, I was hot. I was wearing a woolen shirt and a heavy tunic over it because it had been cold in the morning and we didn't know it would turn out to be a nice day. While the priest was talking, I suddenly became cold. I had been sweating from the heat, but now that sweat was freezing cold. I tried not to let anyone see how my body was shivering, and I pressed my fists as hard as I could into my legs.

I was sitting like that, shrunken into myself, when I sensed that people were staring at me.

It was a strange feeling that I didn't understand—how could someone feel that people are looking at him even if his eyes are closed. Maybe there was some mysterious force in people's eyes? Those looks actually seemed to be touching me, and I couldn't control myself. I looked up to see who was staring at me.

Violanti! Her eyes, as black as coals, were looking at me the way no other person had ever looked at me. I was so surprised that I didn't do anything. I just sat there like an idiot and felt as if there were a thick string connecting my eyes to Violanti's, and only we could see it. That string was stuck to my eyes and drew them to hers. I was shocked that this was happening to me, but I was glad to see that I wasn't shivering anymore. The cold I'd been feeling was gone.

Juan, who was standing next to me and constantly wriggling, dug his fist into my ribs and made a funny face, looking from me to Violanti as if he were asking: What does she want from you?

When Padre Pedro's long sermon was finally over, we walked with Aunt Catalina, Mencia, and Fernando toward the door. Juan was walking next to Mencia and I heard what they were saying. Mencia said, "Our new priest is a wonderful speaker."

And Juan said, "He's right. Why should we all suffer because of a few criminals? Can you imagine how awful it is to spit on the holy cross! How can they do that?!"

I looked behind me and saw that my mother could hardly walk, and my father was supporting her. Their faces were white. But Aunt Catalina looked the worst— her face was actually green. She walked with her head held high, and the black tiara she wore made her seem taller. It looked as if she were walking alone, even though we were all around her. Something in the way she looked scared me. Had she suddenly been struck blind? Because she walked like someone who doesn't see anything.

I saw people saying good-bye to my father, and he responded with a nod of his head.

I heard Juan's happy voice say, "You see, Mencia, a lot of people here already know my father. He helped so many of them during the epidemic."

I was sure that Mencia would be thinking of her own father now, of Uncle Alonso, and she'd be sad, but I couldn't see her face. Fernando was in the way.

"Where are we going?" Juan asked when he saw my parents walk in a direction that didn't lead to our house.

"To Aunt Catalina's," I heard Mother reply.

Juan was the only one who talked on the way. But when we reached the house and my Uncle Alonso greeted us at the door, none of us could control ourselves, and cries of surprise blended with tears of joy.

Chapter Eight
VIOLANTI

"What a strong woman Aunt Catalina is," Remedios said when we got home on Sunday evening. "If I were her, I definitely would have fainted. But Father, you actually controlled yourself very well too," my sister said and smiled at our father. "I watched you while you and Uncle Alonso embraced, both of you so tall and strong, and I thought about how sad it was that Grandfather couldn't see these two sons of his."

Father smiled back at Remedios and said admiringly, "I hadn't noticed how grown-up you've become. You think like a woman now, not like a child. I too sometimes think how sad it is that our parents, mine and your mother's, haven't had the joy of watching their grandchildren grow up. Yes, it would be true to say that Portugal is a land that devours its residents."

"Not its Christian residents," Mother said bitterly, "Our neighbors reached old age. We were the only ones they persecuted. Oh, my poor parents . . ."

Mother left the room and Father went after her.

Remedios bit her lips and grimaced as if she were in pain.

"It's all my fault," she whispered. "Why did I have to mention Grandfather?! I wasn't thinking about Mother's parents."

"You never told me what happened to them, Remedios."

"That's something we don't talk about at home, Manuel. It was a terrible thing. But I suppose if you're grown up enough to know that we're Jews, you can hear about that too. Mother's parents were burned at the stake, Manuel."

"They were burned alive?"

My sister nodded and whispered, "In an *auto de fe.*"

"How old was Mother when it happened?" I asked a long while later, because I couldn't speak before then.

"She and Tereza were very young. Aunt Clara, Catalina's mother, took them in and raised them both."

I knew that, of course, because mother and Aunt Catalina were like sisters.

"Once, I thought that Aunt Clara was our grand-mother, even though we called her Aunt," I said.

"Yes, she was like a grandmother to us, and I was sad when she left Bragança with Catalina. I knew in my heart that she wouldn't survive the hardships of the trip to Spain. And a short time after they reached Seville, Aunt Clara passed away."

Although I was proud that Remedios was talking to me like that, I was sorry I'd asked her those questions. I saw how sad it made her, and I wanted to say something to change her mood.

"Uncle Alonso was so happy when Uncle Lorenzo told him how well father is doing in Seville. Did you hear what he said?"

Remedios looked at me as if she were waiting for me to go on.

"Uncle Alonso said: 'Thanks to you, my brother, it is better for all of us here!' And then he said: 'It is very good that you studied medicine, Rodrigo. There are more than enough merchants like me here. But good doctors are always needed.' Maybe I'll learn to be a doctor when I grow up. Look at how respectfully the Duke treats Father—he sends his carriage here to get him. What do you think, Remedios?

"You know, Father said that if he keeps on earning as much as he is now, we'll be able to move to a new house soon, a bigger one than we have now."

"I'm comfortable in this house," Remedios said. "I've gotten used to it. What we need now are teachers for you and Juan. Diego won't be available to teach you anymore—Uncle Lorenzo needs him at work."

"Do you think father can find teachers who are *conversos*?"

"Any teacher can teach arithmetic, geography, Latin, and literature," Remedios replied, and that's how I knew that they were looking for a Christian teacher for us.

About two weeks after that conversation with my sister, a tall handsome young man came to our house.

Our new maid, Maria, brought him into the living room. (Our former maid, Ana, didn't come back to work in our house after the epidemic. She married a widower whose wife died of the plague and was raising his children.)

"Don Antonio," she introduced him, blushing.

"Ah, this is the teacher who has come to teach the boys," Mother said, and sent Maria to look for Juan.

Antonio and I shook hands.

"Do you like to study?" Antonio asked after we sat down in the small room. That's what we called the cubbyhole off the living room.

"It depends," I replied. "I like to hear stories about things that used to be, interesting things."

"I've heard that you want to be a doctor, and for that, you have to know Latin very well . . ."

"Who did you hear that from?" I asked, interrupting him. Remedios was the only person I'd mentioned it to.

"From your father."

"Ah, my sister told him."

"You have a sister? I thought you were only two boys," Antonio said.

"I have an older sister; she's eighteen. Her name's Remedios."

"Remedios, that's a nice name," Antonio said, smiling. "And now let's hear what you want to study today."

"History. But maybe you should start with my brother Juan?"

"You're the only one here now. What do you know about our Seville?"

"Hey, which one of us is the teacher, you or me?" I said, laughing.

Antonio laughed along with me.

"I would guess that you don't know a lot about our city," he said, shaking his head. "Okay, I'll tell you. It was founded many centuries ago. They say that the strongest man in the world, Hercules, founded it. He was Greek, and he came here by ship. Later, the Phoenicians came. Do you know who the Phoenicians were, Manuel?"

"We decided that you're the teacher," I said with a smile.

"The Phoenicians were an ancient people who lived along the eastern coast of the Mediterranean Sea and who sailed on commercial trips in large ships built of cedars from Lebanon."

I was happy when Juan burst into our study room and chattered to my mother, who was right behind him, "Why is Manuel always the only one everybody teaches? I want to be the first. I deserve it. Manuel already studied with Diego." Antonio and Mother smiled at each other.

"Please join us. We've started with the history of Seville," Antonio said.

"No. I want to study alone with the teacher. Manuel will bother me," Juan cried.

I didn't show how easy it was for me to give up the history lesson, and how happy I was to get out of it.

I took the Latin book Diego had given me and sat down next to the large window, the one that faced Violanti's house.

I started practicing verb declensions, and very quickly found myself lost in thought.

Ever since Alonso came back to Seville, I'd been thinking about him often, especially about the things he told us. How he went to Cádiz disguised in a plain tunic so that if he met people he knew (and my uncle knew merchants everywhere in Spain), they wouldn't recognize him as the wealthy merchant, Alonso Nuñez, and wouldn't turn him in to the people searching for him. The entire time he spent in Cádiz, he was sure that the *Santo Oficio* had sent secret agents to find him. I remembered his description of how strange he looked, even to himself, with long hair and a beard, and I tried to imagine him like that, but I couldn't. Before he came back, he'd had his hair cut and his face shaved, and put his regular clothes back on.

The whole time my uncle was gone, my father had tried to find out what that servant had told the Inquisition, and Melchor Pereira, a family friend who we had known back in Portugal, had helped him. For that purpose, large sums of money had passed from Aunt Catalina, through father and Melchor, to people connected to the Inquisition Court. But none of them had actually gone to hear the testimony, although the Inquisitors spoke about it and we knew that it made accusations against Uncle Alonso.

In Cádiz, my uncle hired people to search all of Andalucía (a region of Southern Spain) for Sancho, but the servant who had spoken out against my uncle was nowhere to be found.

During the search for Sancho, my uncle stayed in Cádiz to wait for news from the people who were helping him. Finally, they came and told him, "Sancho is dead. We found his wife, and she claims she doesn't know anything."

"Bring her here. I'll pay her generously if she agrees

to come," Uncle Alonso told his people, and he forbid them to tell her where she was going and why.

Sancho's wife saw the money, which they gave her in Málaga, the city she was hiding in after her husband died, and she agreed to go with my uncle's people even though she didn't know where they were taking her and why, so she would receive more money.

They brought her to Uncle Alonso's rented house in a suburb of Cádiz—he hadn't gone to live in a village, like our father thought—and my uncle questioned her.

"What did your husband die of?"

"Probably from too much excitement," she replied. "He had a weak heart."

"What did he say in his testimony?"

"How should I know that?!" the woman replied.

"If you talk, I will pay you very well," my uncle promised.

"He said many things, but his testimony was cut off in the middle. I know that because people from the *Santo Oficio* came and asked me to complete the sentence my husband had started and never finished. They said it was my duty to complete it, and if I didn't, they wouldn't allow poor Sancho to be buried and he would go to hell.

"They read the sentence to me: 'I do not believe that Don Nuñez or his family truly belong to the ch . . .' and that's where the sentence ended.

"They asked me what he meant, and I said I didn't know. They questioned me about whether my husband had told me about that family—if they mock the church and obey the commandments of their vile Torah. I said that he never told me anything about that. They asked if he'd ever heard prayers in the Nuñez house that were not Christian prayers; if he'd seen the members of the family working on Sunday and resting on the sixth day; if they ate pork in the Nuñez house."

The woman had answered "I don't know" to all of those questions, and Uncle Alonso believed her when she put her hand on a statue of Jesus and swore that she was speaking the truth.

She said that the Inquisitors demanded that she leave Seville and helped her find a house in Málaga.

"They must have been afraid that I'd find out from Sancho's wife that the *Santo Oficio* had no incriminating testimony against me," Uncle Alonso said. "They hoped to get a confession out of me that would allow them to arrest me for a long interrogation. But I kept repeating that I had no connection to the religion of Moses. And I didn't understand what they wanted from a good Christian like me, who went to church every Sunday, who confessed to the priest regularly, who took the sacraments, kissed the cross and taught his children to love the messiah, his Father, the Holy Ghost and the Holy Mother, Mary."

But Uncle Alonso didn't think his words or the fact that his family had been Christians for generations had satisfied his interrogators.

While he was being questioned, my uncle didn't know that the Inquisitors didn't have any evidence against him except for what they assumed would have been the end of Sancho's sentence. So he decided to disappear and find out for himself what he was being accused of before they actually arrested him.

All of us here in Seville had trembled in fear, I thought, fear for Uncle Alonso and for ourselves, as we had no way of knowing that Sancho hadn't managed to say anything specific in his testimony.

I was sure that it was no accident that Sancho's heart stopped beating the minute he started to say the word "church." It was like what happened with the epidemic—our God saved us from disaster. If we kept on believing only in Him and if we obeyed the commandments of the Torah of Moses, we would remain safe from all evil. That's what I thought.

I was still engrossed in those thoughts when I felt again what I'd felt in church. Something invisible, but real, had grabbed hold of me and was drawing me toward it. I looked up, and it was her—Violanti.

I saw her standing in the window of her house, staring at me with her black eyes.

"*Buenos días*," she called to me.

"*Buenos días*," I replied.

"What are you reading?"

"It's a Latin textbook that I got from my cousin . . ."

"I'd like to see it close up," Violanti said.

"Do you know how to read?"

Violanti made a gesture to show that she didn't.

There was a long silence, and I pretended to be reading the book.

"Manuel, could you teach me?"

"When?"

"Now. I'm alone again."

I didn't answer her right away. I couldn't decide. On

the one hand, I was afraid to go to Violanti's house, and I didn't know why. On the other hand, something drew me there, and I didn't know what.

It was the voice of our new teacher, Antonio, echoing from the small room, that tipped the balance. I did not want to study history.

"Okay, I'll come. But only for a little while. I have to be at a lesson that our teacher is giving soon."

I told my mother that I was going to Violanti's house to show her my Latin textbook. She looked at me in surprise but didn't say a word.

I crossed the alley to Violanti's door, and she was already opening it, her black eyes glittering in the darkness of the hallway. Hanging on the walls of their living room were pictures of the Christian saints. There was one of John the Baptist, of the Holy Mother, of St. Thomas, and a few pictures of Jesus.

As I looked at them, I felt as if Violanti's eyes were trying to pull me away. They flashed with dissatisfaction, with a kind of anger.

"Come, we'll sit down here," she said, inviting me to the armchairs near the window.

I sat down where she told me to, and I saw some rosary beads on the table in front of me. I looked at them, and Violanti said, "Don't you have rosary beads like those?"

"We have different ones. And we also have lots of pictures of the saints, like you do," I said, pointing to the pictures hanging on the walls so that she'd think we were good Christians. As she listened to me talking, that expression of dissatisfaction came back to

Violanti's beautiful face.

"Show me your book," she said quickly, as if she wanted to change the subject.

I gave it to her.

"You understand everything that's written here?" she asked, turning the pages.

"Some of it. Where are your parents, Violanti?"

"Out. Would you like something to eat or drink? Wait for me here, I'll be right back with some grape juice and raisin cakes."

When she didn't come back right away, I went to see what she was doing. The kitchen was next to the living room, where we'd been sitting, but Violanti wasn't there. I went back to my chair and looked out of the window, where I could see into our living room. I hoped that Juan would come to our window so I could talk to him, but I knew there wasn't much of a chance because he was getting a lesson in the small room. Maybe my mother would come to the window. No, she was in the room where she worked on her spinning wheel, and Remedios was there too.

"Where were you?" I asked when Violanti came in holding a tray full of cakes, fruit, and glasses of grape juice.

"In the cellar. That's where we keep the jugs of juice and the fruit," Violanti replied, and pushed away the rosary beads with the tips of her fingers, as if she could not bear to touch them, so she could put the tray down on the table.

While we were eating—the cakes were sweet and crunchy—Violanti said, "Manuel, do you know when I noticed you for the first time? It was about a month after you came to live here. I saw you come out of the house hiding something under your tunic. That made me curious, because you were walking like someone who had an important job to do.

"I waited for you to come back, and it took a long time before you came down the alley. I knew they were worried about you because your mother kept coming to the window looking upset.

"Later, I saw you come back with a very dark boy dressed in rags, and then I was really curious. Tell me, Manuel, where did you go and who was that boy?"

Violanti's eyes rested on me like a heavy sack, and I said to myself that I'd been stupid to come here.

Chapter Nine
A Walk through the Alleys of Seville

Mother sent Juan to get me, and he came right before I started to tell Violanti the lie I'd manage to think of in order to explain why I'd left the house when I went to the slaughterer's courtyard and how I'd met Aldino.

I'm sure that if I'd had enough time to talk, I would have felt terrible. Because when I lie, I never think anyone believes me and I get all tangled up in new lies in the hope they'll be more convincing than the earlier ones. For example, that's what happened to me when I was talking to the new maid, Maria, about the Moors. I'd heard her say that all the Moors are liars and thieves, and that made me mad.

"I don't know any Moors," I lied. "But I've heard of a nice Moorish family that always did good deeds."

"Where did you hear about them?" Maria asked.

"Where? In church!"

"That can't be," Maria declared. "No priest would ever say good things about the Moors, just like he wouldn't say good things about the Jews."

"Who said I heard it from the priest? Lots of people go to church, right?"

"People who say nice things about the Moors? It can't be. Maybe you heard it somewhere else."

"Maybe you're right. It wasn't in church, it was at our friends' house."

"What friends, Manuel? Do I know them?"

I could have said no and gotten myself out of the mess. But I really wanted to convince Maria that I was telling the truth, so I replied, "Yes, they've been here. The Pereiras. Do you remember Melchor and his wife, Leonor?"

"The ones whose son died in the black plague epidemic?" Maria asked.

I nodded, feeling my face turning white with fear. What would happen if Melchor and his wife came to our house and the maid asked them? I tried to calm myself down by saying that maids didn't usually ask their masters' guests questions. But still, it bothered me for a while, until I'd almost forgotten about it, and I was sure that Maria had forgotten it too.

I asked myself, how is that Juan came just when I was about to open my mouth to answer Violanti's questions? And I was sure that there was an invisible hand, our God's hand, in it.

"Manuel," Juan called to me when he came into Violanti's living room gesturing with his hands for me to come. But when he saw the tray on the table, he put his hands down and stood there as if he was waiting for something.

Violanti knew what my little brother wanted, and she said, "Come here, Juan. Have one of the cakes I baked. And maybe you'd like some dates?"

My brother looked at me as if he were asking permission, and when he saw that I wasn't responding, he went to the table and took a raisin cake.

"Only one?" Violanti said, laughing. "Take some more, Juan."

My brother didn't wait for her to say it again. He reached out and scooped up a handful of cakes.

"They're very good," he said, as if apologizing, and hurried out with his loot.

"We still haven't had a chance to talk," Violanti said when Juan and I were standing at her door.

"And we won't," I said to myself. But to her, I said, "We'll talk another time."

We went into our house, and Antonio, our new teacher, asked, "Where did you disappear to, Manuel?"

"He went to his girlfriend's house," my little brother said, giggling. "That girl, she's in love with him. In church, I saw the way she looked at him the whole time. Tell me, Manuel," he asked me, "what do you do to make the girls love you so much?" Then he said to Antonio, "Our cousin Mencia is in love with him too!"

Antonio laughed, but when he saw that I was blushing furiously, he stopped laughing and said to me, "Don't pay attention to what he says. That's what children are like. They always think their older brothers and sisters are better than they are."

"No. Violanti *really* loves Manuel," Juan insisted. "You should have seen what she gave him to eat!"

I asked myself if what he was saying was true. Was Violanti in love with me? Or maybe she only wanted me to talk! But why? Why was she so interested in finding out where I went that day when she saw me going to the slaughterer with the chicken hidden under my tunic? And why did she care about poor Aldino? Will I ever see him again? Where did the monks take him, I asked myself, and what happened to him?

"Come, my young friend, pull yourself together," said Antonio, who had misunderstood the reason I was dejected. "You should be happy that girls like you. As the first epistle of St. John says: 'For God is love.' And you both undoubtedly know the rest!"

My brother saved me from embarrassment when he said, "God loves us, and that is why He sent his son, the savior, to us. I've heard that many times from our priest. I mean from the priest we used to have."

"Very good," Antonio praised Juan. "That is what's written in the New Testament: 'The love of God was made manifest among us, that God sent his only son into the world, so that we might live through him.' And what do we conclude from this? That too is written in John's first epistle: 'If God so loved us, we also ought to love one another.'"

I thought about what Antonio said when we left the house to take a walk around the city. If Christianity teaches man to love his fellow man, why did the pure Christians hate us?

I looked for a way to ask Antonio without making him suspicious of me, and I said, "Good Christians have to love everyone, right? So why do so many of them hate the Moors?"

"Because they are heretics who deny the holiness of our messiah!" Antonio said. "Obviously, we have to hate heretics!"

I wanted to ask why. Why do we have to hate heretics? Aren't they people like everyone else? If they had done something wrong, like our stupid maid says, I could understand that we'd have to be against them. But if their only crime is that they believe in the god of their forefathers, and not in Jesus, I don't think it's right to hate them.

"What are you thinking about, Manuel?" Antonio asked me when I didn't respond to what he'd said. "You must know a Moor. Otherwise, you wouldn't ask that question."

I shook my head "no," thinking that it would be better if he knows as little as possible about me.

"He's lying," Juan said. "Manuel had a Moorish friend. His name was Aldino!"

Oh, if only I could—I'd give that brother of mine a few smacks, I thought.

Antonio looked at me, waiting for an explanation.

"Oh, that boy I used to know. Yes, I forgot all about him," I stammered.

Antonio didn't say anything, and we walked for a while without talking.

"What's the name of that tower over there?" Juan asked, pointing to the tower rising up on the side of the cathedral we were passing.

"That's La Giraldo Tower. Do you want to climb to the top and see the whole city?"

Juan was thrilled with the idea and began running ahead.

"Wait, Juan, first we'll go into the cathedral. I want

88

to show you both the huge cross made from the gold Columbus brought back from the new world he discovered."

Standing at the door, Juan and Antonio crossed themselves. They weren't looking at me, so I didn't. I was glad I'd managed to get out of it. But all of a sudden, I felt my heart pound wildly—maybe someone sitting inside the cathedral, hidden in the dark, had seen me come into the church without crossing myself!

Father had warned me again and again not to act suspiciously in public. He told me that outside our house, we had to act like good Christians. And what Christian goes into a church without crossing himself? At least I should have put my hand on my forehead for a minute and let it slip down, like Father showed me.

I went inside, and no one in the cathedral looked at me.

"It's so beautiful," Juan said excitedly when we reached the gold cross.

"Shh," voices shushed him, and Antonio pulled him by the hand to show him portraits of the saints and the gold decorations and precious stones that were so plentiful in the cathedral.

They walked hand in hand, smiling at each other, and I walked beside them. They stopped near a wall that had beautiful stonework, and Antonio explained to us that it was left from the Moorish mosque that had stood here before it was turned into a church.

But Juan didn't want to hear any more explanations, and he cried, "Let's climb La Giraldo Tower."

Before Antonio could answer, Juan ran outside without waiting for us.

We went right out after him so that he wouldn't get lost in the crowd. And what was my naughty little brother doing? Hiding behind a tree not far from the church, and we passed him by without seeing him. We walked farther on and he sneaked up behind us and let out a frightening roar.

I could see from Antonio's red face that he was angry, and that made me feel very good. Now Antonio would know which of Dr. Nuñez's two sons deserved to be treated well. I'd been feeling that he liked my brother better than he liked me.

The view we had from the top of La Giraldo Tower was magnificent. We could see the large river, the Guadalquivir, that flowed through the city, with many ships and boats on it; we could see the luxurious palaces from above, and our eyes were drawn to the Alcazar, the palace of the Moorish kings who once ruled the city, and the tower next to it.

"I want to climb up that tower too, over there," Juan said, pointing to the same tower I was looking at.

"Oh, you mean the Torre del Oro," Antonio said and smiled, his anger at Juan already forgotten. "You still have strength enough to climb today?"

"I'd rather stay here," I said when I saw that my brother was planning to go down. "The gardens next to the Alcazar are so beautiful, and I see other palaces. What's that one over there, on the other side of the river?"

"It's not exactly a palace," Antonio replied. "It's a fortress, the Triana Fortress, where the *Santo Oficio* holds most of its interrogations. Of course, the Inquisition also has buildings on the eastern side of the river: there, there, and there. But the Triana Fortress is the largest and most beautiful."

Antonio went on talking, but I closed my ears. The word "Inquisition" was enough to stop me from wanting to hear more explanations, even though earlier I'd wanted to ask him the names of all the churches I could see from the Tower. I wasn't even interested anymore in seeing all the neighborhoods of the city from above. (I'd seen my house as soon as we got up there.)

Antonio was busy explaining and didn't notice that Juan had disappeared. I interrupted him, "Where's Juan?" Antonio looked around worriedly. We circled the Tower to see if he was hiding in some corner, as he had earlier.

We didn't see him, so we went down the spiral staircase. People who were coming up slowed us because the steps are narrow and there's not enough room for some people to go up and others to go down at the same time. I felt as if it had taken a long time to get to the bottom. We looked for my brother in the church. We called out his name, we asked people, but he had disappeared.

"He must have gone to another tower, the Tower of Gold," I said, and we started to run toward the *Torre del Oro*.

Suddenly, Antonio stopped and said, "And maybe he went a different way?"

"You don't have to worry so much," I said. "He's not a baby. We'll find him."

"It's easy for you to talk, Manuel, but I'm the person responsible for him, not you. It was stupid for me to take you out for a walk in the city on our first day. I thought you'd enjoy your studies more. That was clearly a mistake!

"Listen, Manuel, I'll go that way and you keep going straight. We'll meet at the Tower," Antonio said, and turned south. He'd almost disappeared past the alley when I heard someone call him, "Antonio, Antonio," the voice echoed through the narrow space.

There was something familiar in the voice, something frightening. Hadn't I heard it once before?

"Oh, Lopez," I heard Antonio call to someone, "help me find a lost student."

Then I couldn't hear their voices anymore, and I started walking straight ahead toward the Tower of Gold. But the voice that called to Antonio stayed with me, and I asked myself again where I'd heard it before.

I was the first to reach the Tower, and Juan wasn't at the entrance. Maybe he meant a different tower, I thought, and I didn't know whether to go up or wait there for Antonio.

I was still trying to decide when Antonio—along with a boy (probably Lopez, I thought)—asked me, "Is Juan here?"

I didn't answer. My tongue was stuck to the roof of my mouth and I couldn't talk. The boy with Antonio was the one who'd stopped me, who'd chased me, when I came out of Don Anton Martinez's courtyard with the slaughtered chicken hiding under my tunic..

Chapter Ten
RECKLESS LOPEZ

It's hard to understand how a boy as mischievous as my brother Juan could have been born into our family. He saw us looking for him and stayed in his hiding place behind a bush, enjoying the raisin cakes Violanti had given him when he came to her house to call me. He'd kept them under his tunic the whole time.

Earlier, I'd asked him to give me one. I knew he was saving a few of them. But he snapped at me, "Go to Violanti and she'll give you as many as you want. After all, she's in love with you!" And now he was feasting on them alone.

Antonio was the one who discovered Juan's hiding place a short while after he'd arrived with Lopez. Now that the "lost boy" was found, Lopez was free to give his attention to me. He looked at me with a frown, trying to remember. "We've met somewhere," he said in his firm voice, giving Antonio a questioning look.

"Oh, I forgot to introduce you," Antonio said. "Manuel, this is my friend Pedro Lopez, but we always call him by his last name."

We shook hands and I quickly pulled my damp

hand out of his. I felt like I was choking, and I prayed he wouldn't remember how and where we met.

"Manuel is the brother of that naughty boy, Juan, and both of them are my pupils. You must have heard about their father—Dr. Rodrigo Nuñez. He became famous during the epidemic. No other doctor in Seville risked his life the way he did to help save the sick."

"They're Portuguese," Lopez said to Antonio.

"Yes, they lived in Portugal before they came to Spain, and we, the people of Seville, are fortunate that they left Portugal and came here," Antonio said to Lopez, then turned to me. "Lopez is the brother of my best and dearest friend, Enrique, may he rest in peace. We were like brothers. A day doesn't go by when I don't think about him and mourn him. He died in that terrible epidemic."

"The doctors didn't help Enrique," Lopez said accusingly.

"They helped everyone they could, and if it hadn't been for Rodrigo Nuñez, my father wouldn't be alive either," Antonio said, taking a piece of cloth from his belt and wiping his face.

So that was how Father met Antonio, I thought. I wondered if what Antonio had just said had an effect on Lopez, who kept scrutinizing me.

"Hey," Lopez cried in surprise, "you're the one we stopped on the street. We thought you were a thief. Tell the truth. What did you have under your tunic? You were hiding something, don't deny it! We chased you and looked for you, but we couldn't find you. Where did you run off to?"

"I went down to the river," I replied through clenched teeth.

"But what were you hiding from us?"

I felt how not only Lopez but also Antonio and Juan were staring hard at me.

It was the raisin cakes my brother had eaten that gave me the idea that kept me from falling into the trap.

"My sister baked some cakes and sent me to bring them to my aunt's house. I knew that if you saw them, you'd want to eat some."

"Remedios, our sister, bakes the best cakes," Juan said. "When you come tomorrow, Antonio, ask her for some. You won't be sorry."

I was amazed at how easily the lie about the cakes came out of my mouth, and thought about the miraculous way the excuse had come into my mind. And I'm usually so bad at inventing lies!

Those miracles must be happening to me lately because I stopped being a Christian. Ever since I learned about my real religion, my life has become interesting and wonderful. That's what I thought, and I felt very relieved.

I looked Lopez straight in the eye without batting an eyelash.

"All of us were sure you stole something," Lopez said, and a smile spread across his face. "Do you remember the friends who were with me?"

I made a face as if to say: Who remembers things like that!

"I'm sure they remember you," Lopez said, chuckling.

"You should take Manuel into your group. He's your age," Antonio suggested.

Lopez looked at me defiantly, waiting for my answer.

"I'm pretty busy, especially now that we've started our studies."

"Still, you should make friends with boys your own age," Antonio said. "And even though Lopez seems reckless, deep down he's really kindhearted."

"If people give me cake, I get very sociable," Lopez said and laughed. "Try me."

"*Bueno*," Juan said, "come home with us. I'm inviting you!"

"*Chiquito*," Lopez teased my little brother good-naturedly, and added with a big smile, "*Gracias.*"

"You'll come?" Juan asked.

"If you invite me, of course I will! I never pass up invitations to eat good cake."

"Lopez likes to joke. Don't take him too seriously," Antonio told us, and drew a circle on the ground with his stick. Then he stuck the stick in the middle of the circle and when he saw where the stick's shadow fell, he decided that it was late and we had to go back home.

Before we left Lopez, Juan repeated his invitation, and again, I had the urge to smack him. Who asked him to mix in? It would be very awkward if Lopez came, and he might even bring his friends, the ones who were with him when they chased me.

"Antonio, do you think Lopez will come to see us?" I asked after we'd left him.

"Only if you ask him yourself," Antonio replied.

It rained for the next few days, and we didn't leave

97

the house. Antonio came every day to teach us, and I knew he felt good in our house because each time he stayed a little longer than he was supposed to. But I didn't guess why—I didn't guess what it was that made him stay for hours.

He'd come before noon and teach us according to the plan we'd made. First, a short lesson with Juan. Then the main lesson with me while Juan studied what he'd learned earlier. At the end of my lesson, Antonio would test Juan on what he'd learned in the morning.

Maria served us lunch in the small room where we studied, and when we finished eating, Juan had another short lesson. My brother was very proud of the progress he was making in Latin, geography, and arithmetic.

I was doing very well too, and when my cousin Federico, who was studying medicine in Alcalá University, came and tested me, he said, "You know enough now to be accepted into the university very soon."

I asked Federico about his studies, and when he told me what his daily schedule at the university was, I said that I'd rather stay home for the time being and study with Antonio. He said that his classes start at five in the morning and end at night after a meeting with the rector (the head of the university), who came to discuss what he'd learned that day.

"I'm studying at a very good university, but even at the University of Seville, a student has to sweat to get his medical degree," Federico said.

I didn't understand why someone who wants to be

a doctor has to learn the Scriptures, for example. Federico told me that he had to become well versed in the New Testament, not to mention the endless prayers, confessions, and religious ceremonies he had to take part in.

I thought about what my cousin, a Jew like me, was going through and how he always had to pretend he was a devout and observant Christian. If they suspected he wasn't, not only would they expel him from the university but they'd also arrest him—along with his family—and interrogate him until he'd been tortured so much that he confessed.

I knew those things because I once asked Diego what they'd do to his brother if they found out he was Jewish and not Christian. My question upset Diego then, and after he answered me, he asked me never to mention that subject again.

That's why I asked my father what the Inquisition did to someone who was interrogated and confessed that he was Jewish.

He'd replied, "If the person asks for forgiveness and swears to be a faithful Christian from then on, there's a chance that they'll give him his life as a gift. But they sentence him to be punished severely, and they confiscate all his property. He has to wear a special robe called a *sambenito*, and he has to stay in prison or under house arrest. And there are many other punishments."

I asked, "And if the person who confesses doesn't ask for forgiveness and says that he wants to keep being a Jew, what do they do to him?"

Father lifted his hands hopelessly and said, "What

do they do to him? They burn him at the stake in an *auto de fe*."

"They burn people for that?"

"Yes," my father said and sighed, "and after terrible torture."

"But why?" I asked in anger.

"Because all the Jews who lived in Spain were expelled one hundred and fifty years ago. Only the ones who were baptized as Christians were allowed to stay. When you're baptized—and all of us were baptized—you are required to be a faithful Christian. Judaism is simply forbidden in this country. Do you understand, Manuel?"

"So what are we doing in Spain?" I asked Father. "Aren't there other countries where we can obey the commandments of our religion?"

"Yes, but we couldn't go directly there because of the great distance."

"Then maybe we can leave now, Father?"

"Leaving Spain is not easy either, Manuel. If we could, we would already have gotten on a ship and sailed to Venice or Amsterdam."

From my lessons with Antonio, I knew where those places were, and I used to sail to them in my imagination.

Oh, I thought, how wonderful it must be to do what you want and not be afraid all the time. I imagined the pleasure the Jews must feel who could openly light Sabbath candles, eat their Sabbath meal together after bathing and putting on clean clothes without being afraid of the servants or the neighbors, fast together on the day of the Great Fast, and pray together to God, the

God of the Jews. Father taught me the *shma Yisrael* prayer, and soon he'd teach me the *amidah* prayer.

Antonio came to teach us on Saturdays too. The only day we didn't study was Sunday. If we'd told him we didn't want to study on Saturdays, it would've made him suspicious.

My parents told me to be careful around Antonio. They were afraid that I would get so used to him that I might let some unnecessary word slip out, or something I did might show him how I really felt about the religious subjects we sometimes studied.

I began to realize that Antonio knew more about the stories of the Christian saints than he did about geography and arithmetic. He taught us about the lives and teachings of the saints whose pictures hung on our walls, and of the ones whose pictures we saw in various places we visited. I also realized that Juan really enjoyed those stories. But I started to get bored during Antonio's lessons. I felt that he kept repeating the same things and was hardly teaching me anything new. That's why I liked walking around the city with him more than sitting in the study room and listening to him tell me something I already knew.

It was on the day of the Queen Esther Fast that I asked Antonio to go out on an educational walk with me. He looked out the window and said it was raining.

"So we'll get a little wet. We're not made of sugar, and we won't melt," I said and wrapped my wool tunic around me. My mind was set on going out.

Antonio protested, and then my sister came over to help me convince him. She knew I wanted to go out so

I wouldn't have to eat.

"You've been stuck in the house for days," she said, smiling at Antonio. "You'll dry up!"

Antonio got up immediately, and I saw from his expression that he was agitated.

"You might be right, Remedios," he said in a hoarse voice and added, "Maybe you'd like to come along?"

"Me?!" my sister cried in surprise. It was not decent for a young woman like her to walk around the city in the company of a man who was not part of her family.

Antonio's face turned bright red, and he stammered, "Ah . . . It's . . . Just . . . With your brothers. You are permitted to walk with your brothers."

Remedios looked at him in confusion, and she blushed too.

"Maybe another time," she said. "I can't today. I have to bake."

"Remedios never lets the cook or the maids bake cakes," Juan said, laughing. "That's why she's always busy!"

We went out, and I noticed that Antonio stood in the alley and looked at the upstairs window to see if Remedios was watching us, and she was.

"Let's cross the bridge today," Juan suggested. "I want to see up close that fortress we always see from far away."

He meant the Triana Fortress, where all the important *Santo Oficio* offices were.

"No, Juan," I said firmly. "I was the one who said we should go out, wasn't I? So I'll pick the place we go to today: Alcazar!"

Antonio agreed with me, probably because he did

not want to go too far in the rain.

We walked close to the houses, which protected us from the rain, and suddenly, the door of one of them opened and a gang of boys ran out. I saw Lopez in the group right away, and I had a bad feeling.

"Oh, here you are," said a firm voice that I immediately recognized as his. "*Buenos días*, Antonio."

The gang of boys with Lopez surrounded us and started whispering to each other as they stared at me.

"Remember him? Manuel?" Lopez asked them.

Antonio looked at me and must have understood what I was feeling. He came over, put his arm on my shoulder and, a smile flitting across his lips, said to the boys, "Well, you must be Reckless Lopez's friends. I've heard you like to have a good time."

"We're a group of Young *Guardas*," one of them said. "And Lopez is our chief!"

"Perhaps you'd like to take Manuel into your group?" Antonio asked, tightening his grip on my shoulder.

The boys sneered, but Lopez walked over until he was standing right in front of us.

"I've already told you once that we'd be happy to have Manuel in our group!"

"And what about me?" Juan interrupted, and his loud question made them break out laughing.

"And what about me?" Lopez laughingly repeated Juan's question. "Drink a lot of milk and eat a lot of meat to grow and get strong. Because we only take in boys who are this tall." He raised his arm and touched my head, saying, "Here, you see, *chiquito*, your brother's the right height."

Chapter Eleven
SHARING THE SECRET OF THE YOUNG GUARDAS

After we left Lopez and his gang, we went home. On the way, Antonio talked to me about Lopez and told me how close he'd been to his brother, Enrique.

"In fact, we were a threesome: three inseparable friends—Enrique, who was my dearest friend; Santiago, the brother of Tomas, who is the same age as you and Lopez and belongs to his group, the Young *Guardas*. And I, who have no brothers, only older sisters. Since Enrique died, I feel all alone," Antonio said sadly.

I told him that if they were a trio, then he still has a friend.

"Ah, Santiago," he said, nodding his head and sighing. "He's a shadow of what he used to be. We used to go out and have such good times together. We'd ride horses, drink good wine, and talk about whatever was on our minds. But now, Santiago doesn't take an interest in anything, except..." Antonio didn't finish the sentence.

"And it's all because your friend, Lopez's brother, died?" I asked.

Antonio shook his head, took a deep breath, and

finally said, "Maybe because of that too."

Juan wasn't listening to our conversation. He ran ahead and stopped next to our house. "Do you smell it?" Juan asked us. "It smells like poppy seed cakes!"

I knew that the fast wasn't over until the stars came out, and it was still early. So as soon as we went into the house, I said that I was very tired and was going to my room.

"You won't eat?" Antonio asked.

"Maybe I'll eat with you later. First, I'll rest," I said and went straight to my room.

Juan said he was starving, and I heard his voice calling Maria, "Quick, Maria, bring Antonio and me some food!"

If it hadn't been for the strong aroma of the cakes baking in the kitchen, I might have fallen asleep. I hadn't slept much the night before—thoughts about the Queen Esther Fast and about the celebration after it kept me awake.

This was my second fast. The first was the Great Fast when we pray most of the day and think about what happened over the last year, and we ask forgiveness for the bad things we did, intentionally or not.

That fast had been easy. I didn't even feel it. But still, I was afraid of today's fast, afraid that I'd suffer, that I'd be very hungry. And I was. But on the other hand, I was proud of myself for overcoming my hunger, and fairly easily at that.

I hoped Antonio would leave early and not interfere with our celebration in memory of the day the Jews of Persia were saved from death. But when the first stars came out and I left my room, I saw him sitting in the living room.

I didn't stop myself from saying, "Are you still here?"

Juan answered for him. "Antonio's waiting for Remedios."

I saw our teacher jump up from where he was sitting as if a snake had bitten him, and he looked like someone caught doing something wrong.

"What kind of nonsense is that!" Antonio said in a harsh voice and looked at the door to see whether anyone but us had heard him. When he saw that we were alone, he said to Juan, "You have an overactive imagination. Now I know why Manuel was angry with you when you talked about all those girls who are in love with him. A boy your age should be interested in more important things!"

Juan looked at Antonio, ashamed, and I was also surprised that Antonio had reacted so angrily. He always spoke to us very nicely. Even when Juan hid from us and then scared us, Antonio hadn't spoken to him so sharply.

We heard the voices of people coming into the house, and I remembered that Melchor and Leonor Pereira were invited to have dinner with us after the fast.

The voices of our guests and my parents, who went to greet them, sounded cheerful. You could feel that this wasn't an ordinary evening. Suddenly, I remembered the conversation I'd had with our maid, Maria, about the Moors, when I told her what I'd supposedly heard in the Pereiras' home about a nice Moorish family. Now I felt as if I'd fallen into a trap. Would the maid dare to ask our guests?

Oh, why hadn't I kept my mouth shut? My parents and my sister warned me not to have idle conversations with the servants, and they were right. But no, I thought, trying to calm myself down, Maria won't ask—she probably forgot!

The guests were still standing with our parents in the entranceway when Remedios came into the room wearing an embroidered dress that suited her perfectly. Her big brown eyes shone above her red cheeks. And her thick black braid, wound around her head like a wreath, gave her a festive look. She looked like a queen that night.

Antonio got up when she came in, and I was surprised to hear the tone of his voice. "*Buenas tardes,*" he said in amazement, as if he were seeing not a woman but an angel or a fairy. My sister returned his greeting in a shy voice and lowered her gaze.

At the same time, our parents' voices were coming closer to the living room, and I could see Melchor and his wife at the door.

Melchor opened his mouth to say something, but when he saw Antonio, he didn't speak and his wife came into the room without saying anything either.

My father saved the guests from embarrassment by introducing Antonio to them. "This is our sons' teacher, and it is thanks to him that Manuel has become so well versed in the sciences. Federico Monsanto, who is a medical student and the son of our relatives, Lorenzo and Tereza, said that this boy of ours will soon be able to begin university studies."

"I'm doing better than Manuel, Father," Juan said, sounding hurt. "He studied before, with Diego, so it's no wonder he knows more."

Even though I heard what my brother said, I had no desire to answer. Something else had drawn my complete attention: the looks that were passing between my sister and Antonio.

Antonio seemed to ignore the fact that he was being talked about. His eyes were fixed on Remedios, but her eyes weren't looking down anymore. Large and glowing, they were looking straight ahead—at him, the dark, handsome young man whose face, like hers, was flushed now.

"Remedios," my Mother said, "you know that our servants are off tonight, and the food cooking in the kitchen needs watching."

Only then, when Remedios went out, did Antonio wake up to see what was happening in the room.

"What holiday is it today?" Antonio asked in surprise.

"Holiday?" Father repeated, and shrugged his shoulders. "Why do you think today's a holiday?"

"I don't know. There's the feeling of a holiday, of something special, in the air."

"It's a holiday for us every time good friends like Melchor and Leonor—whom we've known for years— come to visit," my father replied.

"Do you always study until this late?" Melchor Pereira asked Antonio.

I remembered what Juan had said earlier, that Antonio stayed late only to see Remedios, and wondered how he would answer.

"We took an educational walk in the city today, so we had to reorganize the order of our lessons," Antonio replied.

"Today? In the rain?" Leonor Pereira said in surprise.

"Manuel wanted to . . ." Antonio began saying, but Juan interrupted him. "We met some boys who want Manuel to join their group. They call themselves the Young *Guardas*."

Everyone stared at me, waiting for an explanation.

"Antonio knows them better than I do," I said, and all eyes turned to him.

"They're the same age as Manuel, and I only know two of them. One is named Tomas de Trujillo. His brother, Santiago, is a good friend of mine. The other is Pedro Lopez. His brother, Enrique Lopez, was my dearest friend, who died not too long ago in the plague epidemic."

Antonio didn't understand the meaning of the silence, the deathly silence, that fell on us when we heard those last words of his. He didn't know that the Pereira family had also lost a son to the epidemic. He looked at the window, as if help would come from it, to save him from the terrible sadness that filled the room, and he said quietly, "The sky is full of stars. It must be very late. I'll go get my tunic."

"I'll go with you," Juan said and looked at Mother for her permission.

110

"Go, Juanito, and then to bed."

"But . . ." my brother started to say something, but didn't finish. The look that Father gave him silenced him on the spot.

"Tonight of all nights, that young man had to stay late," Mother grumbled after Antonio and Juan had left. "That was not our arrangement with him. I don't understand what's happened to him lately that makes him want to stay later and later. It could only mean that he's expecting us to pay him more money!"

"Why should you speak so badly of him, Ines?" Father asked. "Antonio is a bright and likeable young man, and he does his job faithfully and diligently. Isn't that true, Manuel?"

I didn't know how to reply, and since Melchor and his wife were also looking at me, I asked them—instead of answering—the question that had been bothering me, "Have you seen our new maid, Maria?"

"We've sent the servants away tonight so they won't be here for our holiday meal," my mother replied instead of them.

My question surprised Father, and maybe he was angry at me for not answering his question.

"What do the servants have to do with Antonio?" he asked, demanding an answer from me.

I told them about the conversation I'd had with Maria and how afraid I was that she'd find out I'd lied to her, and my father said, "How many times have we told you, Manuel, to hold your tongue!"

The words came out of my father's mouth angrily, as if he were hurling stones at me.

"Please, Rodrigo, let's not spoil the holiday," Mother said, putting her hand on Father's cheek to soothe his anger.

And as if to calm things down even further, Remedios came in to tell us that our meal was ready.

We sat at the table that was covered with a white tablecloth, and Father filled a wine glass to the brim, raised it, and said, "Tonight we must drink our fill. Blessed be God, our God, King of the Universe, who created the fruit of the vine."

We said "Amen" and drank the thick, sweet wine Father poured into our glasses.

"We say a slightly different blessing," Leonor said.

"That is the blessing my grandfather taught me," Father replied. "But I saw in the prayer book you showed me, Melchor my friend, that it is not exactly right. Perhaps someday we will be able to read our holy books openly and pray together to God."

Remedios got up from the table and went to the window.

"What's wrong, Remedios?" Mother asked, alarmed.

"I just wanted to see if the curtains had moved, Mother."

"Remedios is doing the right thing," Leonor Pereira praised her, "I do the same thing at home—I constantly check to see that the windows are well covered. Heaven help us if anyone sees us like this, sitting together for a holiday meal. After all, the Inquisition knows the dates of our holidays."

"Manuel, what group of boys was your teacher talking about?" Melchor Pereira now brought up the Young *Guardas* that we'd spoken of earlier.

"Yes, I also wanted to ask you about that," Father said, "what sort of group is it?"

"I don't know. And I was very surprised that they asked me to join. I once met their leader, the one they call by his last name, Lopez. In fact, today was the third time I saw him. The first time, he and his friends chased me, and it was a miracle that I got away from them. I told you about it: how they called me names and said I was a Jewish convert . . ."

"Ah," my mother said, remembering the incident, "that was when you took the chicken to the slaughterer and we waited so long for you to come back."

"Yes, it happened after I left Don Anton Martinez's courtyard."

Once again, worry dampened the joy of the holiday, and Father sighed and said, "The name of that gang— Young Guardians of the Law—is enough to terrify me. What do those boys want with one of ours!"

"They decided to ask me to join them because of Antonio. He knows them well and he told them how you saved his father and he praised you so much, Father, that they were influenced by him."

"You should keep away from them, my son," my father said with a sigh.

"I only hope that Manuel doesn't act in a way that arouses their suspicion," Melchor Pereira said. "I hope he doesn't make those Christians angry and give them a reason to gang up on him."

"What do you suggest, Melchor?" Father asked.

"The only way is to pretend. If Manuel refuses to join them, he will make them angry. So he must pretend to agree, and see how it works out. It might only be a boys' game!"

That's what Father's friend said after thinking about it for a while, and then he added, "In the years I've been living in Seville, I've learned that gangs come and go, and only one thing never changes—the Holy Institution of the Inquisition. The *Santo Oficio* is the only thing to fear."

Again, it was Mother who reminded us of the holiday meal we had sat down to eat together. "Please, at least tonight, let's drink and be happy and forget that cursed Inquisition. Fill the glasses, Rodrigo. Remedios will be serving the roast fish in a minute."

The meal we ate that night consisted of the same dishes we'd eaten after the Great Fast. Fish, vegetables, and eggs. But after the Great Fast, we didn't drink much wine or eat cake.

Mother and Remedios had baked special cakes for that evening: triangular cakes filled with poppy seeds and raisins. When I asked about those sweet, crunchy cakes, I remembered that Juan had promised to give Lopez some of the cakes Remedios baked, and I chuckled to myself. That's something he'll never get! I didn't know how wrong I was.

The next day, while Juan was studying with Antonio in the small room, I sat in the living room trying to memorize passages from the Acts of the Apostles from the New Testament because that was what Antonio had told me to do. A noise coming from the alley made me get up and go the window. I didn't see anything at first, and I was about to go back to where I'd been sitting when I saw someone running down the alley. Had I seen that boy before? I asked myself. And then another boy ran down the alley, and him I knew—it was Lopez.

I was very curious about what they were doing, and I waited impatiently to see what would happen next. But after Lopez got to the other side, nothing happened. I knew that the boys were still in our alley, very close to our house, because I hadn't seen them leave.

I waited a while longer, and finally, I couldn't control myself any longer and I went outside. Even before I got past the gate, I could see them standing across the way, close to the wall of the corner house. They saw me too, and Lopez waved his hand for me to come over. When I got there, I saw that there were three others with them.

"We can't tell you what we're doing here," Lopez told me in a low voice. "We can only tell you things after you join our group and take the loyalty oath."

"I'm ready to join now," I said.

"*Bueno*," Lopez said, and turned to his friends. "What do you think, amigos?

Three heads nodded, but the fourth boy looked at me with open hostility.

"I told you what I think," the hostile-looking boy said.

"With all due respect to you and your brother, Santiago, who was responsible for forming this group—the majority rules!" Lopez said to him firmly and decisively. Then he turned to me and asked, "Can we have the swearing-in ceremony in your house?"

"You want to come now, with the whole gang?" I replied with a question.

"There are only five of us."

"I'll go ask, and then I'll tell you."

At the door, I met Remedios, who was on her way out. I told her, and she said she'd stay home to help with the refreshments.

I went back to where they were waiting near the gate and blithely asked them to come in.

Chapter Twelve
WHERE IS LEONOR DE GOVILLA?

"We have exactly the same pictures in our house," said Balthazar, the youngest member of the Young *Guardas*, as we walked past the pictures of the Christian saints hanging in the hallway.

Juan came running out of the study room with Antonio right behind him.

"I see, Manuel, that you've joined Lopez's group," Antonio said, not hiding his satisfaction at seeing the boys in our house.

"*Buenos días*, Antonio," Lopez said. "And how are you, *chiquito*?" he asked Juan.

"I am not little," Juan protested. "And soon I'll be a member of your group too. You promised me, Lopez, that you'd take me in!"

"And this must be Remedios," Lopez said, smiling at my sister, who was standing at the living room door. "Your little brother promised to let me taste the cakes you bake."

"Here, I've prepared some for all of you," Remedios said, pointing at the table in the room, where a pitcher, some glasses, and a plate of cakes were waiting.

We went into the living room, and Remedios went back to the kitchen. Antonio stopped at the door and didn't come in. He stood there looking in the direction my sister had gone in.

"Your sister really does know how to bake cakes," Lopez said, holding a piece of poppy seed cake in his hand, "and you, Miguel, pour me something to drink from the pitcher."

Miguel hurried to do the group leader's bidding, and then Antonio came in, his face shining.

"Manuel and Juan, what do you think about canceling our lessons for today?" Antonio asked us.

Juan cheered with happiness, and I nodded in agreement. But I was wondering why our teacher was canceling lessons without discussing it with our parents. In all the commotion, I didn't noticed when he went out, and I didn't see Remedios any more that day.

"Now for the swearing-in ceremony," Lopez said when only the boys, Juan, and I were left. "Please bring us a New Testament, Manuel."

"I'll get it," Juan volunteered and came back with the book and some rosary beads, which were in our house as a decoration.

"Very good," Lopez praised Juan. "Manuel," he said to me in a commanding voice, "kneel down with your face toward me. Put your hand on the holy book and repeat after me: I, Manuel Nuñez, swear allegiance to the group of Young *Guardas*. I will readily fulfill every mission the group asks me to perform. I will not reveal the principles or activities of the group to anyone, and I will be loyal to it with all my heart!"

I repeated what Lopez said, word by word.

"Get up," Lopez said, gesturing with his hand as if he were lifting me up. "Cross yourself there, near the statue of Jesus, and repeat these words: I swear my allegiance to the group, and I will never betray it!"

I did what he said, and as we went back to the boys sitting around the table, Lopez patted me on the shoulder and said, "I'm glad we have someone like you in the group. From now on, you have the same rights as all the members. And the same obligations, of course. I'll be the first to shake your hand to show that you are now a member of our group, and then you'll give all the boys a strong handshake."

I shook Lopez's hand and then went from one boy to the other, until I got to Tomas, who had been sitting with his head down the whole time and hadn't touched the refreshments on the table. I extended my hand to him, and a while passed before he touched it lightly with his own, his face twisted in disgust.

Lopez rebuked him. "Tomas, don't forget that all the obligations we have taken on ourselves apply to you too! Get hold of yourself. You do know that everything we do is for you!"

Juan, who was present during the ceremony (probably because Lopez didn't want to insult him by asking him to leave the room), asked, "Why is everything you do for Tomas?"

"Only members of our group have the right to ask questions," Lopez replied. "From now on, Juan, you'll have to wait till you've grown up enough to be a member."

"Oof, maybe we can get out of here now?" Tomas grumbled, and he got up to leave.

"Wait, Tomas. First we have to thank our hosts. Manuel, where is your lovely sister?"

"I'll go get her," I said. But Maria, the maid, told me that Remedios had gone out. Mother heard me calling Remedios and came in.

"How much older she looks," Lopez joked when he saw my mother standing at the entrance to the living room.

"That's not Remedios, that's my mother," Juan said and ran to her while all the boys except Tomas laughed. He still looked furious.

"So, you are the Young *Guardas*," my mother said, smiling. "Welcome to our home."

"We're just leaving," Lopez said, still laughing.

"Well then, go in peace."

"Are you coming with us, Manuel?" Lopez asked.

"Where are we going?" Balthazar asked in surprise, "I thought that . . ."

Pasqual, standing next to him, must have pinched him so he would be quiet because Balthazar let out a cry of pain and shut up.

Mother interrupted the conversation and said that she needed me to run an errand for her, saving me from having to answer Lopez's question.

The boys left and I asked my mother what errand she wanted me to do. "There is no errand, Manuel," Mother replied. "All I wanted was to keep you from going out with those boys. My heart told me it would be better for you to stay home this morning. Besides, you have to study!"

"But Antonio is gone," Juan said.

"Where to?"

"We don't know. He said he wouldn't teach us today."

Mother raised her eyebrows in puzzlement and then, gesturing that it didn't matter, she said, "Then you'll study without him."

Juan said he was going out to the courtyard to see what the rain had done to the flowers in the clay pots, and I stayed in the living room.

Why had Pasqual silenced Balthazar? I asked myself, and what were the boys doing in our alley anyway? Maybe it had all been planned so that I'd go out and bring the whole gang into my house.

No, I thought. It was only by chance that I happened to see Lopez run down the alley. He couldn't have known I'd see him. After all, he'd snuck in, and the boys who were standing behind the wall didn't want me to see them. No, I'm sure it wasn't planned. They must have wanted to follow me, and when I saw them, there was nothing they could do but take me into their group. But why were they spying on me? What did they expect to see in our house?

I should've gone out with them. The mystery scared me more than being with them would. Even if that Tomas tried to hurt me—I could see how much he hated me—the others would help me. After all, I was an equal member of the group, with all the same rights. But what if that was just a trick?

They could be in the alley right now, waiting to see

if any of us leaves. Mother said she was sending me on an errand, and here I am, staying home and not leaving. What will they think?

Disturbed by those thoughts, I went to the window and looked behind the curtain at the alley. It seemed empty. I opened the window wide and stuck my head out, whistling to myself to hide my emotions, to see whether someone out there really was watching me.

And I did feel curious eyes fixed stubbornly on my face. I felt the weight of those eyes on me even before I looked up from the alley straight into the window of Violanti's house.

A strange feeling flooded me. On the one hand, I wanted to get away from those eyes—to move back, close the window, and pull the curtain. But on the other hand, they drew me toward them as if they were magical ropes, and the words Juan once said, "Violanti's in love with Manuel," echoed in my ears and made the blood rush to my burning face.

"Manuel," I heard Violanti's voice calling me. "Manuel."

I let my head turn so I could see her.

"Can you come over? Please come. There's no one home, and I have to tell you something."

I nodded and looked around the alley again to check whether any of the boys were there, and when I saw that it was empty, I closed the window and ran out of the house. I crossed the alley and before I even touched the bell, Violanti opened the door.

"What did you want to tell me?"

"I'll tell you right away, but first tell me, what were

those strange boys doing in your house? Are they your friends, Manuel?"

Again, those questions of hers, I thought angrily. What a curious girl she is! Because of her, I was in an embarrassing situation again, the way I'd been when she asked me where I was going when I went out with the chicken under my tunic. Was she spying on me? And what right does she have to demand that I answer her questions, the questions of a bored girl with nothing else to do but look out the window and see who goes in and out of her neighbors' houses.

What am I doing here? I'll go and I won't come back again. Violanti won't be able to tempt me into coming here again. She won't be able to make me talk, not even if she offers me her raisin cakes and other good things to eat.

Violanti gave me that intense look of hers while she waited for me to say something, but I didn't open my mouth. It stayed closed.

"You don't have to tell me anything, Manuel. I'm sorry I even asked you. Come in, we'll sit in the living room and I'll bring you some candied fruit."

"Thank you, but I don't want to eat. I have to go. I'm planning to be accepted to the university medical school, so I have to study a lot."

"But your teacher's gone. I saw him leave with your sister. Oh, Manuel, you have to warn Remedios." The words came out as if on their own, against her will.

"Warn her?" I asked in surprise. "About what?"

"Oh, Manuel," Violanti cried in pain, and I had that strange feeling again—as if I were drawn to her and away from her at the same time. "You don't know how much I want to talk openly to you, but I can't. All I can tell you is that she has to be very careful. I have an older sister too. Her name is Leonor, and she . . ."

"She what?"

Violanti looked down and slowly bent her head. She stood like that and began to weep silently, her full red lips trembling. I felt my hand move automatically toward her, and I pulled it back at the last minute. God help me if I stroked the head of a girl who was not a member of my family, I thought and swallowed. I suddenly felt as if I were crying with her, and I ran outside to keep myself from getting carried away with the emotion that was flooding me.

I stood in the alley like someone who had been through a frightening ordeal, trying to calm my pounding heart and silence the voices arguing in my head. I was ashamed for running away like that, and I scolded myself. But I also heard another voice inside me: You did the right thing Manuel, that was the only escape. Violanti is not your relative. You have no obligations to that girl!

I went home, took the New Testament and opened it to the Acts of the Apostles. Finally, the eighteenth chapter, the one that tells about the Jew of Alexandria, whose name was Apollos. He was a Torah scholar who was baptized a Christian and taught Christianity in the synagogue where the Jews prayed. "He powerfully confuted the Jews in public, showing by the scriptures that Christ was the messiah."

I'd believed that once too. I'd been sure that Jesus

was the messiah, the son of God. When my father told me that we were Jews, he argued with me until I accepted his opinion that God couldn't have a son. But what do I care if the Christians believe that Jesus is the messiah, like I once believed? Why all those arguments about what's true and who's right? Let everyone believe what they want and that's that.

But the Christians won't let us believe what we want to believe. If they suspected that we didn't believe that Jesus was the messiah, they'd lock us in dark cellars and use their instruments of torture on us. That's why we're so afraid.

Violanti looks frightened too. What is she afraid of? She told me to warn Remedios. What should I warn her against? Why didn't Violanti tell me what happened to her older sister? It was a mistake to run out of her house like that. I should have stayed to ask her. I know she wanted to tell me things.

I was still deep in thought when I heard a horse galloping down the alley and the sound of wagon wheels. I ran over to the window and saw the wagon stop in front of our house, and out of it stepped Aunt Catalina, Mencia, and Remedios.

I was glad to see Mencia run and skip to our gate. She looked so nice in the red wool dress she was wearing. I went out to greet her, a big smile on my face.

"It must be weeks since you were here last," I said to my little cousin.

I said hello to my aunt, who was coming in now. Remedios was the last to get out of the wagon. I wanted to tell her what Violanti had said, but something stopped me—maybe it was her very pale face, and maybe it was something else that had to do with Violanti. I don't know. But whatever the reason, I did not tell her.

Mencia came to my room with me and started telling me about her new dolls. She was practicing her sewing by making dresses for them. "I'm learning how to embroider too," she told me proudly. "I'm almost finished embroidering a tablecloth."

I was bored by Mencia's chattering, and when Juan came and started talking to her, I was glad I didn't have to continue the conversation.

I went back to the living room and started reading the Acts of the Apostles again, but my sister's image kept flickering before my eyes, and I felt that I wasn't taking in anything I was reading.

I asked Aunt Catalina about Fernando, and she said he was helping his father, Uncle Alonso, selling in the fabric store. I said I was going there to see him and got permission from my mother to come home late.

Fernando was glad to see me and said, "Let's take a few minutes to sit down and talk a little. I've been working since the morning and need a break."

But in the meantime, more customers came into the store, and I saw that Fernando wouldn't be able to get away to talk to me. I asked Uncle Alonso if I could help with anything, and he said I should come another day when there were fewer customers. Then he'd explain the things I needed to know before they could let me sell cloth.

I decided to go to the market, to Uncle Lorenzo's

spice store, even though I didn't know whether he was there, because he has stores not only in Seville but also in Madrid, Toledo, and other cities.

In the store, I saw my cousin Diego, who used to teach me science and who now was learning the spice trade with his father.

Diego was very busy too. Not only wasn't his father in the store and he had to supervise the two salesmen they employed, but he also had negotiate with the spice merchants who came to buy spices so they could sell them elsewhere.

I was sitting on a large box near the door and inhaling the delicious aromas of the spices when Pasqual, one of the boys who'd been in my house that morning, passed by.

I said hello to him and he said hello back, and even though he looked surprised, he said he was on his way to Lopez's house and asked me if I wanted to go with him. I went with him, slightly anxious because I didn't know what Lopez would say about my coming there, but I was glad too. It's good to know that you have somewhere to go, that someone wants you to go with him.

I was surprised at how happy Lopez was to see us. He praised Pasqual for bringing me along and said, "You see, Manuel, thanks to fate, we meet from time to time so that we can do things together."

What things? I asked myself, because I was too embarrassed to speak.

"And the first thing you can do for the group is to find out the address of a woman who lives on your street. You probably know the de Govilla family..."

My face must have shown that the name was more than familiar to me, because Lopez suddenly stopped talking and looked at me hard before he went on. "You're friends with Violanti, Violanti de Govilla, aren't you?"

"Friends?"

"Yes, Antonio told me that you went to visit her. Well, we have to find out where Leonor, her older sister, disappeared to. And you're the only one who can do that, Manuel. But don't tell anyone what your mission is. Remember your oath!"

"But why do you need her?" I asked. "What's your connection to Violanti's sister?"

"You'll find out all about it, Manuel, when the time comes," Lopez promised me. "When you bring us her address, we'll tell you."

Chapter Thirteen
A SHOCKING DISCOVERY

I wanted to go home, but Lopez wanted me to stay. "What's the hurry?" he asked, laughing. "Violanti won't run away!"

"How do you know?" asked Pasqual.

"She never leaves her house. God only knows what she does there all the time, alone," Lopez said.

"I'd really like to know where her parents go. Every time we try to follow them, we lose them. That old couple sneaks away like a pair of cats," Pasqual said, laughing and ignoring the signs Lopez was making for him to stop saying those things.

"What do you say we go for a ride in our wagon? Look, my father's putting the horse back in the stable," Lopcz said.

We helped harness the horse to the wagon, and Lopez asked me to sit next to him.

"And you, Pasqual, sit in the back and watch to see whether any of the gang is in the streets we drive through," Lopez commanded the amiable Pasqual, who obediently followed all of his orders.

"Giddiyap," Lopez raced the horse, and the wagon

leaped so quickly down the street that I was afraid its shafts would break. "Where would you like to go, boys?"

At first I wanted to ask him to drive to my house, but then I changed my mind. I was enjoying the drive with them, and besides, I didn't want Violanti to see me with them. I knew she spent her time at the window, and she would definitely see us coming.

"We'll go wherever the wind takes us," Pasqual cheered from the back of the wagon.

"Whatever you say," Lopez replied and raised the whip above the horse without touching her. "Oh, dear horse of mine," Lopez began to sing. "Oh dear horse of mine, anywhere you take us will be fine."

Suddenly, he pulled hard on the reins and the wagon stopped. A boy who looked about Antonio's age was running to catch up to us.

"*Buenas tardes*," Lopez called to the young man. "*¿Que tal?*"

"Did you find her?" the man asked without saying hello to Lopez.

"Be patient, Santiago, we're doing everything we can to find her!"

"Listen, Lopez, I've already given you money and I'm ready to give you more. But you have to find her quickly. And what are you doing? Enjoying a nice wagon ride! Is this the Young *Guardas*? I'm surprised at you, Lopez."

"Trust me, Santiago. I know what I'm doing. This isn't just a nice ride, like you think, and you should meet our new member, Manuel," Lopez said, pointing at me.

But Santiago didn't even give me a look. "Yes, I heard all about it from Tomas," he snapped and went on his way without saying good-bye to Lopez.

"Giddyap," Lopez roared to give vent to his anger.

"Hey, stop," a desperate voice called out from behind. And then Pasqual gave a cry of pain.

I grabbed Lopez's arm and yelled, "Stop the horse!" and without waiting for the wagon to stop, I slid into the back and tried to help Pasqual, whose leg was squashed between two boards that had come loose from the wild jerking of the wagon.

"Oh, my leg, my leg," Pasqual screamed with pain when Lopez and I pulled the two boards apart.

Pasqual's leg was blue and swollen.

"Let's lay him down on his back and take him to my father," I said to Lopez. "I think he's home now."

We drove to my house and my father, who was home already, came to the wagon. By the light of a torch, he bandaged Pasqual's broken leg, using a board as a splint.

"You have to stay lying down, my boy, until the bone knits, and you must keep off that leg for two weeks," my father instructed Pasqual and gave him a painkiller and a salve to rub on the injured leg.

"My father will come to see you tomorrow, Dr. Nuñez, to pay you," Pasqual said and moaned.

"That's not necessary," my father told me. "I don't take money from my son's friends."

As if on signal, Lopez and I raised our eyes to look at Violanti's window, and we both saw her standing there, although only a faint silhouette was visible.

"Ask her," Lopez whispered to me.

"Not today," I whispered back.

"Tomorrow!"

"Maybe."

The torch lit Lopez's tense face and his hard look as he repeated, "Tomorrow!"

I didn't reply to that "tomorrow," which sounded like an order that was not open for discussion.

Pasqual sobbed with pain.

"*Gracias*," Lopez said very politely to Father. Then he turned back to me and said firmly, "*Mañana*."

Lopez had the horse almost galloping but stopped himself from driving the wagon as wildly as he'd done before. Father put his arm around my shoulder as we walked slowly to the gate of our house.

"Are you seeing him again tomorrow?" he asked worriedly.

"I don't know. Antonio's coming tomorrow, and we're going to study."

"That boy said '*mañana*.' "

"He was talking about something else, Father."

I knew that even if I'd sworn my allegiance to the group, I couldn't hide anything from my father.

"What was he talking about, Manuel?"

"The group is looking for Violanti de Govilla's sister, and they gave me the job of getting Violanti to talk so we can find out from her where she is."

"Why?"

"I think that a young man named Santiago, who's the older brother of one of the boys, wants to know. By the way, Santiago is the one who's Antonio's friend, and if it hadn't been for Antonio, I wouldn't be part of the group."

Father suddenly dropped his hand from around my shoulders, and I saw his face contort in anger. Then worry took the place of anger and deepened the lines in his forehead.

"It's all my fault," he said, hitting his hand on his forehead. "How easily I fell into the trap they set for me, and I dragged you into it too, my son!"

I didn't understand a thing, and Father explained, "Antonio asked to become your teacher, and I—in all my naiveté—was glad to give him the job. I believed that by doing so, I could achieve two things. You and Juan would study, and the people in Seville would get to know us as good Christians. Because Antonio's family is one of the most respected in the city, and his father is close to the Cardinal. I thought that having Antonio in our home would help us, but it looks like I was mistaken."

"I still don't understand," I said. "What trap did Antonio set, Father?"

"He was sent to us to get you into the Young *Guardas*. Mother told me that those boys came to our house this morning and Antonio—instead of teaching you and Juan—got up and went. He didn't want to be involved so we wouldn't suspect that he'd planned it that way, so you'd have no choice but to join the group."

"But why do they need me, of all people?"

"Because we are neighbors of the de Govilla family!"

"What should I do now, Father? Should I go and

question Violanti?"

"If only I knew why they want her," Father said, shaking his head in frustration.

Mother's voice calling us ended our conversation and brought us into the house. But not before Father asked me not to say anything about what we'd discussed, not to share our concern with Mother and Remedios for the time being.

At dinner, Juan couldn't stop talking about Mencia: what she told him and what he told her and what games they played.

"I like Mencia more than all my other cousins," Juan said. "She's the nicest one in our whole family."

"Mencia really has changed since Uncle Alonso came back from Cádiz," Mother remarked. "She feels safe now, so she's happy."

Remedios sat there silently, and Mother noticed that she wasn't eating.

"What's wrong, Remedios, are you ill?" Mother asked her worriedly.

Father was immersed in his thoughts and didn't notice what was going on.

"Rodrigo," Mother said to him, "I think Remedios is ill."

Father got up heavily and felt my sister's forehead.

"No," Father said, shaking his head. "She's not ill."

"And what about you?" Mother asked. "You've eaten practically nothing, Rodrigo!"

"I ate, Ines," Father replied distractedly and pushed his plate away. Then he gave Remedios a long look and a cloud of worry settled on his forehead. "Where were you today, Remedios?"

"What?" my sister asked as if waking up from a dream. "What did you ask me, Father?"

"Where were you today?" Father repeated his question.

"Me? I went to Aunt Catalina's, and from there I came back here with her and Mencia. Why do you ask, Father?"

Father made a gesture to show that he had no answer and looked at me as if he wanted me to say something.

Did Father know that Remedios had left the house the same time Antonio did? Violanti saw them going out together—perhaps Father had seen them too.

I tossed and turned all night, and I couldn't fall asleep. What would I do the next day? Would I go to Violanti and try to get her to talk about her sister? What if she started crying so bitterly again? Would I run out of her house like I did before without getting any answers?

I suddenly understood why she'd asked me about the group. She must have seen the boys hanging around the alley, and it was only natural that she'd want to know what they were doing. And maybe she sensed that they were following her and her parents.

Where *did* her parents disappear to every time?

I wanted to know the answers to all those questions popping up in my mind not so I could tell Lopez and the gang, but for myself. And I was really curious to know the answer to the most important question. Why was Santiago looking for Violanti's sister? What did he want from her? Why was it so important for him to find her?

The thought of how I'd left Violanti when she was so upset kept bothering me. How could I go to her now—after acting so shamefully—and question her?

In the morning, when Antonio came, I saw that his face was different from the way it usually was. He looked as if he hadn't slept all night either. His expression grim, he ordered me to recite from the Acts of the Apostles, and when I couldn't, he made a face as if he was dealing with a slow pupil.

"Go and read again what you read yesterday, but try to remember something, at least one of those wonderful stories," he said to me and began teaching Juan arithmetic.

I stood at the living room window waiting for Violanti to appear in the window across the way, but today of all days, I didn't see her there. I waited and waited. I pulled the curtain aside and opened the window. I stuck my head out and pulled it back in a few times so that Violanti would see me doing it. She'd be curious to see what was happening in the alley, and when she looked out, I'd see her. But she didn't come to the window all morning.

Antonio called me again, to test me, and when he realized that I didn't remember a thing about the Acts of the Apostles, he got angry and said I wasn't worth the money my parents were paying for my lessons.

It seemed to me that he was looking for an excuse to send me away. I asked myself if this was his way of allowing me to go to Violanti.

Every once in a while, Antonio would leave the

small room where Juan was and come into the living room, supposedly to see if I was studying. I say "supposedly" because I felt that he wasn't really interested in whether I was reading or not. He did come over to me, but he barely looked at me or the book in my hand. He kept glancing toward the kitchen, as if he were waiting for something, and then he'd go back to the study room looking sad, as if he was disappointed.

After Antonio had gone, I saw almost the entire group of Young *Guardas* in the alley: Lopez, Miguel, Balthazar, and Tomas. Only Pasqual was missing. They stayed in the alley for quite a while, but this time they weren't acting like spies. They spoke in loud voices, and they seemed to be doing it on purpose so I'd hear.

I listened and heard one of the boys say, "I'm positive he didn't do anything. That Manuel won't be any help to us." I had no doubt that it was Tomas, my enemy.

I was afraid they'd come and pull the bell, so I worked up my courage to go out to them.

"Finally," said Miguel, who was the first to see me come out of the gate, and the boys hurried over to me. Only Tomas stayed where he was.

"Did you go to see her?" Lopez whispered, and there was a hush in the entire alley.

I shook my head.

Lopez's face got red. "You promised!"

"I watched from my window to see if she was home, and I'm sure she went out. I didn't see her all day," I said in my defense.

We could hear Tomas's disdain from a distance: "You're just wasting your time."

"Don't pay attention to him, Manuel," Miguel said, pointing to Tomas. "He'll find out that he was wrong about you!"

"We'll go now and come back tomorrow," Lopez said. "And don't sit around doing nothing, Manuel. This is very urgent, and when you bring us the address we asked for, we'll tell you everything and you'll see how important your mission was!"

I watched the boys leave. How confidently they walked down the alley, how light their steps were. They were so carefree. As longtime Christians, they could do whatever they wanted and no one would investigate them. How lucky they were, how easy it was for them!

I was jealous of those boys. In my heart, I wanted to be like them. But I knew that wish would never come true.

I was about to go through the gate when a slim figure appeared behind the corner house, and I knew right away that it was her—Violanti. Without thinking, I went right over to her.

We both stopped. Her face was white and her eyes burned like blazing coals.

"Are you one of them?" she asked, and I knew who she meant.

I shook my head, then whispered, "I'm pretending." She made a signal for me to be quiet.

While we were still standing in the alley, hidden in the darkness that was beginning to shroud the city, we heard someone coming. We listened and I recognized my father's footsteps.

"Wait here for me," I said. "I'll be right back."

I ran to my father and told him that I'd just seen Violanti and would try to talk to her.

"Where will you be?" my father asked.

"I don't know. But don't worry about me."

I went back to Violanti, who was waiting for me.

"Want to go for a walk?" I asked her.

"Where to?"

"The river."

I didn't think she'd say yes. I thought that, as usual, she'd ask me to go to her house with her. And that's what I prepared myself for. So I was surprised when she said, "Yes. Let's go to the river. There's less chance that people will hear us there."

Tense and watchful, we took side roads, not speaking until we got to the river, the Guadalquivir.

I led Violanti to the tree where I'd hidden from Lopez and his pals, the tree where I met Aldino, the Moorish boy.

It's too bad that we'd become separated. Aldino was such a nice, good-natured boy. We could have been friends, I thought, sighing.

"Why are you sighing?" Violanti asked.

I told her.

"This is the first time you've ever told me anything," Violanti said, and waited for me to continue. I knew what she really wanted to hear, but I kept quiet.

"Tell me about those boys you're friends with, or at least pretend to be friends with. They've been hanging around our alley for a few days, and I thought they were waiting in ambush so they could follow us. My parents noticed them too. Do you know their names?"

I told her their names, but they didn't seem to mean anything to her.

"One of them, Tomas, really hates me," I told her. "And his brother, Santiago, is my teacher's best friend."

Now I could feel a change in Violanti.

"I knew it," she whispered in a trembling voice. "I knew Santiago had something to do with it. And did they send you to find out where my sister Leonor is?"

I didn't answer.

"So that's it. That's why you suddenly agreed to talk to me."

"No, Violanti," I protested. "I wasn't planning to question you so I could tell them what you said. All I wanted was to find out what Santiago wants from your sister. Why does he need her address?"

"He loves her, and there was a time when she loved him too. But now, it's over. My sister married someone else, but Santiago doesn't know that. He's hoping to get her back, and we're afraid of what he might do in revenge. His father has a lot of influence in Seville. Oh, Manuel, we don't know what to do," she said, and her body began to shake from weeping.

This time I didn't stop my hand from reaching out to her. Violanti stopped crying and looked at me with wide-open eyes that glittered with stars. "If only I knew that I could trust you, Manuel!"

"I won't tell anyone," I promised her. "I'm ready to swear."

"But you swore an oath to those boys, didn't you?"

"It wasn't a real oath."

"How can I tell a real oath from a false one?"

"Oh, Violanti, I can't explain it to you," I said, full of despair because I couldn't tell her that the only real oath I'd sworn was to God, the God of my forefathers!

"Your family is Portuguese, isn't it?"

I nodded.

"And all the Portuguese are New Christians," Violanti said.

"Please, Violanti, stop!" I cried, my voice choked.

"But I'm . . ." Violanti started to speak, but didn't finish.

"You're Jewish too?!" I exclaimed, stunned. But I suddenly realized what I'd said, and my heart stopped with terror. Was this a trap she'd set for me?

"My parents didn't want my sister to marry a Christian. They married her off to a Jewish boy, Shimon Prados . . ."

When I heard Violanti's words, I stopped being afraid. I had no doubt that she—like me—believed in the religion of Moses, and this was such a shocking discovery that I was almost completely overwhelmed. All I remember is this: I put my arms around Violanti, and we held each other for a long time as if we'd found something precious we had to protect with our bodies so it wouldn't fly off and vanish.

Chapter Fourteen

AT PASQUAL'S HOUSE

What a difference there was between the way we were when we walked to the river and the way we were when we came back. On the way there, both Violanti and I were filled with doubts, schemes, and most of all—fear. We walked together, but each of us was preoccupied with our own worries.

But on the way back, we walked next to each other but it felt like we were a single body with two heads and one soul, a soul filled with joy. I had never felt such happiness before. All the riddles were suddenly solved, and the beautiful girl didn't seem strange to me anymore. Now we truly understood each other and cared about each other.

My head was so full of thoughts about her that I couldn't fall asleep, and that was my second sleepless night in a row. But if I'd been tortured by frightening nightmares the night before, this night was filled with sweetness—as if Violanti were still beside me.

I wasn't worried anymore about what I'd say to Lopez when he asked me if I'd questioned Violanti. She'd told me what to say, and I was practicing it. "I went to the de Govilla house, but Violanti wouldn't talk to me. I must have insulted her unintentionally, and she made her parents tell me that she wouldn't see me, no matter what." I'd practiced saying those words so many times that I almost believed them and they almost made me sad.

If telling this to Lopez and his boys made them break off with me, that was fine, I thought. And if they still thought of me as a member of the group, it would make it easier for me to find out things that could help Violanti's family.

I planned to tell my father right away about the discovery I'd made about Violanti. But when I got home, they told me that he'd been called out to one of his patients. I didn't know that it was Pasqual's father, who'd come in a wagon to take him to see his son, who was in pain.

At breakfast, Father told me about Pasqual and said I could go with him that morning to see the injured boy. "I told him you might come," Father said. "He's bored all by himself, and he seems like a friendly, kind-hearted boy. I don't understand why he joined Lopez's gang."

"So I won't study with Antonio today?"

"Your teacher will find himself with no students today," Father said and chuckled. "Juan won't be home either. He and Mencia are going to Córdoba with Alonso. My brother has urgent business there, and he offered to take the children with him."

I knew that it wasn't Uncle Alonso who'd suggested the arrangements that would keep Antonio out of our house today. But it was a good plan—after all, why would he come here if his pupils weren't going to be here?

On the way to Pasqual's house, I thought about how glad I was to have the chance to tell Father about Violanti. I wonder what he'll say when he finds out, I thought, biting my lips in anticipation.

To my surprise, Father wasn't the least bit surprised by what I told him.

"I assumed that was the case, but I wasn't sure. I've already asked about that family. I asked Alonso and Catalina, and also Lorenzo and Tereza, but they didn't know for a fact that the de Govillas obeyed the commandments of Moses.

"Now," he added, saying something so unexpected that it hit me over the head like a blow, "Now you must avoid all contact with Violanti!"

"But Father, I told you that we swore an oath to each other," I protested. I felt as if a fire were burning my face and smoke were choking me.

"And you will keep that oath," Father said, adding in a firm voice. "You will keep it in your heart. It is a precious possession. But no one must ever suspect that you two are close friends. Heaven help us if anyone finds out."

I was so upset that I barely understood what my father told me about the danger the de Govilla family was in because Leonor had been in love with a Christian. He might take revenge on them through the Inquisition when he found out she was married to someone else.

"Listen to me, Manuel," Father took hold of my chin and lifted it so he could look me in the eye. "When the Inquisition puts its hand on someone, everyone who has any connection with that person gets dragged along too. That is why you must not have any contact with Violanti. Swear to me that you won't try to talk to her and that you will avoid any attempts she makes to talk to you!"

"Why? I can always say that the Young *Guardas* sent me to talk to her."

"But you said you found a way to keep from carrying out the mission they gave you. You decided to say that Violanti refuses to speak to you."

"I'm changing my mind. I'll keep playing my role as a member of the group," I said quickly, so Father wouldn't think of anything to say against it and forbid me to see Violanti.

"Then you will have to question Violanti and find out where her sister is hiding," Father said to me, his tone sharp.

"They won't know what I talk to Violanti about. I'll tell Lopez that I need time because Violanti doesn't trust me yet," I said.

"And will they believe you?"

"They won't have any way of checking it."

"You're not a good liar, Manuel, and when you get entangled in the lies you tell, they'll get the truth out of you. They'll torture you," Father said and looked at me with a face full of sorrow.

"They're not part of the Inquisition. They're just a bunch of boys who want to find out something for the brother of one of their members. He gave them money to do it, and they're playing at being *guardas*. None of it is serious, Father!"

I took a deep breath.

"You might be right, and you might be wrong. It all depends on how hurt Santiago is. If he isn't badly hurt, perhaps in the end, he'll stop looking for Violanti's sister. But since he's formed a gang of detectives he's willing to spend his money on, I'm afraid that he's not taking the matter lightly."

My father's words sounded very convincing, but I refused to believe that Violanti and I were in danger. Father had mentioned the Inquisition and said that Santiago might take revenge through it. Of course, I knew about informers who gave information about people to the Inquisition when they wanted to take revenge on them, but what could Santiago tell the Inquisition about Leonor and her family?

I asked Father, and he said that giving testimony was enough. "If Santiago gives damaging testimony about Leonor to the Inquisition, even if he makes it all up, Leonor will be called in to be interrogated, and so will the members of her family. And you know, Manuel, the methods the Inquisitors use in their cellars are designed to get confessions. As a doctor, I can tell you that it is difficult for a person not to confess, even if he has committed no crime. When a person's body is being crushed in the stocks or by other instruments, he does not have a great deal of control over his tongue.

"Someone tied to a machine lined with nails that stretches his body and makes holes in it will probably—

before he faints—incriminate even the person he loves most dearly," Father continued. Then he added, "Remember, one of the first things the Inquisition does is to make a list of all the people who had any connection to the person being interrogated."

We reached Pasqual's house and the maid took us to him.

"I'm so glad you came, Manuel," Pasqual said happily when he saw me. "I thought Lopez would come to see me, but no one from the group came!"

"They assume you have to rest," my father said to Pasqual as he examined his leg and wound a piece of cloth covered with a mustard salve around it.

"No, they're not even thinking about me. There's only one thing they care about—finding the woman Santiago loves. Tomas told us that his brother would give us each a whole *real* if we complete the mission. I could buy a lot of things with a *real*. Did you find out anything, Manuel?"

I shook my head and said, "I went to her house, but she wouldn't talk to me. I must have insulted her, unintentionally."

I felt as if I were being forced into saying those things because they were what my father wanted to hear, and I said them for him.

Father glanced up from Pasqual's leg and gave me a look of affection and respect. I knew that he was saying to himself: How proud I am of Manuel; he's so mature for his age. I'd already heard him say things like that when I gave up on what I wanted and did what he wanted. But the sense of gloom I'd felt when we spoke on the way to Pasqual's house stayed with me, and it was even stronger than before.

Will I really never be able to see Violanti again? I thought in despair, and then said to myself that I had to cheer up because we'd probably find a way to meet.

"I'll leave you two alone," Father said after binding Pasqual's leg to the board so that the broken bone wouldn't move.

"I'll be home in an hour," I told my father before he left.

"No," Pasqual protested. "Please, Manuel, promise you'll stay with me at least till lunchtime. We'll eat together and then you can go," said the smiling boy with the curls that fell onto his forehead.

"But I'm fussy about food," I said quickly. "I only eat vegetables and fish, and fruit and cake."

"Don't worry, Manuel, our cook will make whatever you ask for!"

I brought a stool close to the couch Pasqual was lying on so I could hear what he told me about his childhood, which he spent in this house where he was born, and about his friends and his plans for the future.

"I'm going to be a *regidor* like my father," he said. "I'll work for the citizens of Seville. I'll build luxurious buildings and plant gardens . . ."

Pasqual stopped in the middle of a sentence and asked me to go to the window. "I hear familiar voices. Is that Lopez?" he asked.

I could already see Lopez's tall figure near the gate, and with him were Miguel and Tomas.

I drew back without realizing what I was doing.

"Who do you see? Is it Lopez? I know his voice!" Pasqual said.

Luckily for me, Pasqual didn't see how frightened I was.

"They finally remembered me," Pasqual said. "Who else is with Lopez?"

I told him and noticed that my voice was shaking.

"Are you cold, Manuel?"

I nodded, even though a wave of heat was running through me and making my face burn.

"You can put on my wool tunic; it's over there," Pasqual said pointing to a chair.

I put Pasqual's tunic around my shoulders so he'd think I really was shivering from cold, not from fear.

Very soon the boy I'd seen from the window was standing at the door, and I moved back into a corner of the room, fooling myself into thinking that no one would see me.

"*¿Que tal, amigo?*" Lopez asked, walking quickly to the couch Pasqual was lying on.

"Pasqualito," Lopez said affectionately and pushed Pasqual's curls off his forehead.

Tomas and Miguel also went over to the couch and shook Pasqual's hand. They still didn't notice me.

I didn't want them to see me like that, hiding in the corner, but I knew what I'd do when they did. I planned to say "*Buenos días*," but the words just stuck in my throat.

"I was beginning to think you wouldn't come to see me," said Pasqual. "And if it hadn't been for Manuel— hey, where are you? Come over here . . ."

When the boys heard this, a look of surprise came over their faces and they all turned to look at me in amazement. Lopez was the first to recover, and when he spoke, his firm voice sounded amused. "Manuel, Manuelito, of all of us, you're the one who got up early to come and visit poor Pasqual!"

Miguel laughed at the tone of Lopez's voice, and Pasqual also smiled. Only Tomas looked serious. His expression said it all very clearly. What are you doing here? But he didn't open his mouth.

"I asked him to come," Pasqual explained. "My leg hurt so much last night that I couldn't fall asleep, so when Manuel's father said he'd come to examine me this morning, I asked him to bring him. I was so bored lying here alone all day."

I thought I heard Tomas whisper to himself, "Those people push their way in everywhere."

"Stay and have lunch too," Pasqual said. "I invited Manuel, and I promised he'd get the special foods he likes."

"Oh, I see that you and Manuel are good friends already, very good friends," Miguel said, smiling.

"Maybe you both can let yourselves relax and have a good time. You, Pasqual, can't be of any use because of your broken leg. And you, Manuel . . ." Lopez stopped speaking and looked hard at me.

I didn't say anything.

Lopez shrugged and said, "We'll come for lunch Pasqual, after we complete our mission. That'll be a good reason to celebrate."

"And now," Lopez turned and spoke to me, "now

let's hear what you've been up to, Manuel."

Trying to speak confidently, I said, "I went to the de Govilla house . . ." The room was suddenly silent. I took a deep breath and shrugged helplessly. "She, I mean Violanti, wouldn't talk to me."

"That's a lie," Tomas said, leaping toward me. "He's lying."

I thought he was going to hit me, so I moved back. The other boys didn't move. I felt four pairs of eyes piercing my body like needles.

"Why wouldn't she talk to you all of a sudden?" Tomas challenged me.

I didn't say anything.

"Manuel told me that he must have insulted her," Pasqual said, coming to my aid.

"You're so stupid," Tomas snapped at him. "An idiot who believes everything! Can't you all see? Those *marranos*, those converted Jews are all against us. I told you there was no point in taking that mongrel into our group." Tomas said to Lopez and Miguel, pointing at me. "We wasted time because of him. I told you we couldn't trust those *conversos*. And you let one of them lead you around by the nose.

"None of you care that my brother is suffering. You take his money and enjoy it, and he wears out his shoes searching. He spends all his time wandering through the streets looking for her. He doesn't sleep, doesn't eat, doesn't drink. Our mother is losing her mind with worry about Santiago, and I have to stand here and listen to the fairy tales this liar tells. Well you can stay here and listen to this garbage. I'm leaving."

Tomas didn't wait for his friends. He stormed out of the door without a backward glance.

"Wait," Miguel cried after him. "I'm coming with you."

"Stop, Tomas, and both of you wait for me in the alley," Lopez ordered Miguel before he left.

That amused smile came back to Lopez's face, and he said, "You see, Pasqual, we're making sure you don't get bored. And you, Manuel, forget what Tomas said. He says those things because he's worried about his brother. And now you have to prove to him that he was wrong about you. If you want to stay and have lunch with Pasqual, please do, but right after that, go back to your neighborhood and pay a visit to the de Govilla family. I'm sure you'll know how to make the girl talk."

Chapter Fifteen
THE ADDRESS IS KNOWN

Pasqual tried hard to make me feel good in his house. We had a friendly conversation and he told the maid to have the cook prepare the best fish, vegetables, and cakes. You would think I was an important guest.

I tried to pretend I was enjoying myself, but I felt awful. Even though I tried to forget what Tomas said, the words *marranos* and *conversos* kept echoing in my ears, reminding me that I was alien, different. Even though Pasqual was very friendly, I felt that I was in a place where people like me were not wanted.

But even more upsetting than the feeling that I was an alien were the frightening thoughts of what would happen when I left there and went home. Only this morning, Father told me not to go to Violanti's house, and now, after what Tomas said, I would have to go there.

I want to see her so much, I thought. I have to talk to her. She's so smart, she'll probably think of a way out of this mess.

When I thought about Violanti, I had a strange new feeling I couldn't define, a feeling of something magical, something soft and delicate.

Pasqual was talking and I was thinking about other things, mainly what had happened the night before by the river, when my heart suddenly filled with pity that brought tears to my eyes. What will happen to Violanti and her family if Santiago finds Leonor?

Pasqual stopped talking and looked at me in surprise. But it took me a while to notice it—that's how caught up I was in my thoughts.

"Manuel, are you that upset?" Pasqual asked, and I saw from his face that he was frightened. I shook my head.

"Tomas doesn't know what he's talking about. Don't think about him, Manuel. Try to understand him. He feels bad because of his brother, and he's looking for victims to take his anger out on. It's wrong, especially when he does it to you, Manuel. I know that if you could, you would find out where that girl is.

"What I don't understand," Pasqual continued, "is how love can make a person so miserable! Let's say the girl stopped loving him and that's why she decided to disappear—and by the way, I'm sure she must be in a different city—is that a reason to carry on, to get so angry and turn the world upside down looking for her?! I don't think anything like that will ever happen to me!"

My thoughts wandered to Violanti again. What would happen to me and how would I feel if she suddenly disappeared?

But how could I compare the two cases, my train of thought went on, I didn't find out I loved her until yesterday! But still, if she disappeared on me for no reason, I think I would take it very badly.

After eating a good lunch at Pasqual's house, I went home and was surprised to find Antonio there.

"Oh," he greeted me excitedly, "I'm so glad you came home, Manuel. Lopez was at my house about an hour ago. He came to tell me something that will probably make you very happy. You don't have to bother with the mission the Young *Guardas* gave you. They found the address they wanted so much. My friend Santiago found it himself.

"From now on, we can go back our regular lessons, Manuel. Juan's not here today, so we can move ahead quickly. I think you're having difficulty with theology. I've asked you several times about the Acts of the Apostles, and you couldn't answer!"

I was confused. The news Antonio told me, pretending to be indifferent, stunned me because of the threat it held, and it raised a mountain of questions I wanted to ask.

I remembered what my father had told me in the morning, about the possibility that Santiago might take revenge on the de Govilla family when he found out that Leonor was married to another man. What did Tomas's brother know about Leonor? Had he already spoken to her? Perhaps he still didn't know she was married.

Antonio took the New Testament out of his bag, opened it to the Acts of the Apostles and started to read out loud. I didn't hear a word he was saying. I sat across from him, stunned, and his words flew around me.

"Manuel," Antonio said, stopping his reading, "are

you listening?"

"I thought we wouldn't have any lessons today, Antonio."

"You had a day off yesterday, and I thought you'd want to move ahead so that you could be accepted into the university."

"I'm tired."

Antonio's expression turned grim. I could tell I was making him angry. Why is he so anxious to teach me? I asked myself, or is it only an excuse to stay in our house?

"Maybe we could talk instead of studying," I suggested.

I saw Antonio's expression clear.

"Of course. What would you like to talk about?"

"Tell me again what Lopez said," I asked.

"Ah, I see now what's been keeping you from studying," Antonio said with a chuckle, then repeated what he'd told me earlier.

"But where did your friend Santiago find Violanti's sister?"

"He saw her near the river. She was with some people, so he hasn't spoken to her yet. But he found the house she lives in, near the river. She must have relatives in the area. So you see, Manuel, her parents wasted their time trying to hide her from him. Love, my young friend, finds a way!"

Antonio blushed when he said this about love, and even his ears were red. He tilted his head as if he were listening to something, and shifted in his chair. "Maybe, Manuel, we should go back to studying?"

I shook my head.

"Have you seen Remedios?" I asked.

When I said my sister's name, Antonio's face got all red again, and his eyes glazed over. He shook his head.

"Do you know where she is?" he blurted out, sounding like this was a question he shouldn't be asking.

"I just came home, and you were here before me," I replied.

"Your maid opened the door for me, and I think that except for her and the other maid, no one's home," Antonio said, looking at me as if he expected me to say something.

I averted my eyes and kept quiet. I wanted him to go so I could run right over to Violanti's house and tell her what Antonio had said.

We sat there in silence. Antonio got up and went to the window. He came back to where we were sitting. He picked up the rosary beads and looked at the statue of Jesus, and his lips began moving in silent prayer.

I thought about how to trick him into leaving. If I said I was tired and going to rest, he wouldn't keep sitting here in the living room alone. But that wouldn't be polite. The only way to get him out of here, I thought, is to go out with him. We'll walk for a while, and then I'll pretend I'm tired. Antonio will let me go back alone and I'll go straight to Violanti's house.

"Antonio," I said, and he stared blankly at me. Then he suddenly straightened up, refocused his eyes, and said he had to go.

"I'll come tomorrow, as usual," he said as he started to leave.

"But Juan's in Córdoba."

"It doesn't matter. I'll teach you," Antonio said and left.

I rushed to the window. The curtain on the de Govilla window was pulled down and stretched to cover every inch of it. Had the thoughts I'd had in Pasqual's house come true? Had Violanti disappeared too?

For a minute, my heart seemed to stop beating, then began pounding like crazy.

Maria, our maid, came in to ask if I wanted to eat alone because it looked like Mother, Remedios, and Father would be coming home late.

But I could hardly hear her. The drum pounding wildly in my chest filled my ears and I ran to the door, then across the alley to Violanti's house.

I pulled the bell, and when no one answered, I banged on the door with my fist.

I stopped for a minute and listened. There was no sound coming from inside the house.

I went back to banging on the heavy wooden door.

I heard a window open. I looked over and saw that it was the neighbor—an old woman I knew only from sight. Her white hair was all tangled and her beady eyes stared at me with curiosity and suspicion.

What's wrong with me, I thought in desperation. I forgot the rules of caution I'd been taught from the time I was a child! Here I was, doing something that would arouse suspicion. The old lady would ask herself: What's that boy's connection to the de Govilla family that makes him bang on the door like a madman?

I wasn't worried about myself. I was afraid that my recklessness would cause Violanti trouble, that the neighbor would suspect I was there because something had happened to her and her family.

Now, because of me, the nasty rumors would fly. They'd say: The boy came and banged on the door of the de Govilla house like a madman! It can only mean that something's going on there . . .

I stood in front of the locked door for a while, and then I went wandering around the alleys of the neighborhood. I went from one to the other until it started to get dark, and then I went home. Lamps lit the windows, and I hoped my parents and my sister were home already. But only Remedios was there.

My sister and I hadn't talked for a while, and I had the impression she'd distanced herself from me. She used to be very, very close to me once—I'd thought of her as a kind of second mother to me and a friend who told me things and listened to what I told her.

Now we were sitting together in the living room and talking about everyday things. I asked her where our parents were, and she said they must have gone to visit Leonor and Melchor Pereira.

I told her what happened in Pasqual's house, but I could see that she was barely listening to me. It seemed very strange to me. Remedios had always been interested in what happened to me, and now, when I was telling her really shocking things, like the way Tomas had attacked me, she just nodded and said with a dreamy expression on her face, "*Sí, sí.*" As if she were only asking me out of habit to tell her what I did after I left Pasqual's house.

"I came home and found Antonio here . . ."

When she heard the name Antonio, Remedios sat up straight and I saw that she was suddenly alert. Now she was looking at me as if she really saw me. And she was attentive and interested. She leaned forward to hear me better, and she didn't look tired anymore. She was wide awake now.

I suddenly remembered what Violanti had said— "You have to warn your sister"—and I looked for the right words to tell Remedios what I was just beginning to understand.

What could I tell my sister, who was six years older than I am? Who was I to warn her? After all, she knows what happened to Leonor de Govilla. Why can't she figure it out for herself?

I told Remedios what Antonio said to me and what I said to him, and I added that he was looking for excuses to be in our house. I waited for her to say something that would help me tell her what else I was thinking. But Remedios stayed quiet and thoughtful.

I was disappointed.

We sat in silence and my thoughts wandered back to Violanti. Where was she? I had to speak to her urgently. I had to tell her that Santiago knew where her sister lived so she could warn her in time. If only I knew where she might be!

I went to bed before my parents came home. I fell asleep right away, but woke up in the middle of the night with a heavy heart. I was worried about Violanti. I would give anything to see her, even for just a minute.

It was so important that she know.

When I couldn't fall back to sleep, I went into the living room, to the window across from hers. With shaking hands, I moved the curtain aside. Was that a dim light there, in her window? Or was I imagining it? The drum began pounding in my chest again.

The noisy pounding rising from my throat to my ears shut out the sound of steps that came from behind me. And the hand that fell on my shoulder almost made me faint. At the last minute, I stifled a scream.

"I whispered, 'Manuel, Manuel,' but you didn't hear, my son," my father said, his voice bringing me back to my senses.

"Santiago found out where Leonor de Govilla lives," I blurted out, still rattled. "We have to warn them."

"Calm down, my son," Father said, stroking my hair.

"Father!" I said loudly, barely able to keep myself from shouting. "Let me go there!"

"I'll go," Father said. "You stay here."

Father went to put on something warm. Even though spring was on the way, the nights were still cold.

From the window, I saw him cross the alley and disappear into the courtyard of Violanti's house. A few minutes later, I saw him come out of the courtyard gate and I ran to our door.

"They didn't open the door?"

"If they're home, they're sleeping now and can't hear. I knocked on the door lightly so the neighbors wouldn't hear, but there was no answer."

"What's going to happen now, Father?"

"We have no way of knowing that, Manuel. And now you should go to sleep. Tomorrow I'll go to Pasqual's house and you can come with me. We'll talk on the way, and you can tell me all about what happened today."

"Go with you to Pasqual's house? But I was there today until after lunch. And Antonio's coming to teach me tomorrow."

"Antonio?" Father said in surprise. "I told him you wouldn't be having any lessons this week!"

"He came here and waited for me—at least, that's what he said, that he was waiting for me. Lopez had been to his house to tell him that his gang could stop looking for Leonor de Govilla, and Antonio came to tell me that. He wanted to teach me today too, but I said I was tired. He finally left, even though he didn't want to, and he said he'd come back tomorrow."

"If that's the case, you really should come with me to Pasqual's house," Father said. "Good night, Manuel."

I started to go my room, then turned back to the living room and sat down by the window. I felt so dejected, as if the weight of the world were lying on my shoulders. A few months ago, when Alonso was missing, the whole family worried about him, all of us together. But now, I had no one to share my worry with. I was alone.

I imagined Violanti coming toward me in the alley, and I was running to her and catching her in my arms. The thought was enough to make my blood rush through my body with excitement. But the excitement died down immediately. What would Santiago do when he found Leonor and discovered that she was married to someone else? And what would happen to her family?

Chapter Sixteen
THE EASTER PROCESSIONS

When Antonio came to teach me, Father greeted him with these words: "Manuel is ill today."

I could hear their conversation from the room I was in, and I tried to listen.

"I'm not surprised," Antonio said. "He looked very confused yesterday. He couldn't remember anything we studied, and he was pale. Perhaps I should sit with him to cheer him up?"

"Thank you, Antonio. But I think it would be best for him to sleep as much as he can."

"When is Juan coming back?" Antonio asked.

"We'll let you know," Father said, adding, "but we will pay you your wages in full. It's not your fault that one of my sons is ill and the other has gone away."

"There's no need to pay for work that has not been done, Doctor. I will not take any money from you for the days I don't teach."

They spoke for a while longer, and then I heard the front door close and Antonio's steps echoing in the alley.

I was so thankful to my father for getting me out of

studying today and for saying I didn't have to go to Pasqual's house.

But I knew that this couldn't go on for long, and I asked myself what would happen in the future.

That day, Juan came back from Córdoba full of stories about the Roman bridge he walked across with Mencia and Uncle Alonso, about the windmill and the huge cathedral, about the towers and the parks.

He asked about Antonio and was sorry we wouldn't be studying for the next few days. I think he liked Antonio and his lessons very much.

On Sunday, the whole family went to church. I looked for the de Govilla family and saw that their seats were empty. But I did see Lopez, Miguel, Balthazar, and Tomas, who didn't look at me. The other boys gave me a friendly hello and Lopez showed the most enthusiasm about seeing me.

Padre Pedro, our priest, spoke about Easter. He said that all the boys would take part in the Easter processions carrying displays with statues of Christ, the Holy Mother Mary, and other saints. We would also be helping decorate the church for the holiday.

Antonio was in church too. After prayers, he came over to us, and I saw Remedios catch her breath and turn pale. Right then, Mother started talking to her and Father and Antonio tried to have a conversation, which was not easy, because Juan kept interrupting them. My little brother was so glad to see Antonio and so anxious to tell him about Córdoba that Father and Antonio could barely hear each other.

Father told Antonio that it would be best to renew

our lessons after Easter because I would be busy preparing for the processions and Juan would be staying at Aunt Catalina's house till the holiday.

No matter how hard he tried, Antonio couldn't hide his disappointment. He looked sideways at my sister, but Mother pulled her over to where Aunt Tereza and Uncle Lorenzo were standing, and when she looked in our direction, all she saw was my face, because Father blocked Antonio with his body.

That Monday, we started rehearsing for the processions. We practiced carrying the heavy wooden platforms that would hold the statues. The platform I helped to carry showed the scene of Jesus' crucifixion. I think it was heavier than the other platforms because of all the statues on it. And it was very wide. We could barely get it through the alleys when we practiced carrying it through the neighborhood.

We picked it up and carried it with the help of poles that rested on our shoulders. Lopez and I, along with eight other boys, picked up and held the same pole. Miguel, Balthazar, and some other boys carried the pole in front of us. I was glad to see that Tomas was on the other side of the platform.

At first, we practiced during the day, then at night. We turned on the lights that lit the platforms, and the statues looked so beautiful.

When we were standing around resting, I told Lopez how beautiful I thought our platform was with the lights on, and he said, "Wait till the platforms are full of flowers. Then you'll see the most beautiful sight in the world!"

I didn't know where they got those thousands of flowers. Their fragrance and colors were intoxicating. They told us to cover the floor of the platform with red carnations as a symbol of the blood of Jesus that spilled from the cross. We fastened the flowers to each other and lay them very close together on the floor until they turned into a blood-red carpet. They also gave us white carnations to decorate the sides. I understood that the white would bring out the purple, blue, and black of the velvet robes draped around the statues on the platform.

It wasn't only the flowers and splendid clothes that attracted the eye but also the glittering jewelry made of gold and precious stones that the statues wore.

Pasqual, whose leg had almost healed but was still weak, came to watch us rehearse, and he was the one who asked about Santiago. I didn't dare raise the subject.

Lopez signaled for him to come over to us and, speaking quietly so Tomas couldn't hear, said, "My heart goes out to him. From the day he found out that the woman he loved betrayed him and married someone else, he's turned into a shadow of what he used to be. All he cares about now is revenge!"

"How will he get revenge?" Pasqual asked.

"Santiago found out that her husband is one of the *judaizantes*, and she probably is too," Lopez replied.

"So that's why her parents broke them up and married her off to someone else so quickly," Miguel said, reaching a conclusion that was met with nodding heads.

"Oof, those *cristianos nuevos*. I can't stand them. They are all liars!" Balthazar cried.

Pasqual and Lopez exchanged glances, but avoided looking at me.

"Did he give testimony to the Inquisition yet?" Miguel asked Lopez.

"Yes, and Santiago hopes they'll burn his former love at the stake," Lopez said.

"Very good," Balthazar said, rubbing his hands together, "that's something we have to see!"

"My father told me that he once saw an *auto de fe*," Miguel told us. "My father says the crowds went wild with excitement and he was carried away with excitement too. Just imagine, you see the sinners roasting in the fire, the way they do in hell."

"It would probably scare me," Pasqual said.

"You'd go and enjoy it like everyone else," Balthazar told him.

I tried not to listen. But it wasn't only that my ears heard what they were saying. Their words were etched deep in my soul. The fear that I had almost managed to push away (Lopez and Pasqual were so friendly to me that I felt a sense of security), that fear came back and took control of me. But now it was even bigger, the kind of fear that completely surrounds you like a black cloud. The kind of fear that makes you shrivel up because you feel you're different. And you know that if the same thing that happened to the de Govilla family happens to yours, no one will be able to help you.

The boys talked about the fire that burned the sinners, the heretics who didn't believe in the Christian messiah. I smelled smoke in the air. We were considered heretics too. And what if someone wanted to take revenge on us and found a way to expose us, to tell the Inquisition who we really were?

I tried not to think about Violanti. Thinking about her made me desperately sad.

I couldn't stand the thought that I'd never see her anywhere but in my mind. I was sure that's what would happen, that we'd never see each other again.

I knew what happens when someone gives incriminating testimony to the Inquisition. Either the Inquisition arrests the ones who've been accused or can't locate them because they've found a good place to hide. But one way or the other, I wouldn't see Violanti. That's what I was thinking.

I was glad to be busy with preparations for the Easter processions. I was tired after rehearsals, and my shoulder hurt from carrying the heavy load. The tiredness drove away my thoughts and worries, and I even slept pretty well at night.

My parents complained that I didn't eat enough. But now of all times, now that we had enough money to put the best food on our table, I had no appetite.

Father said that even if I had no appetite, I had to force myself to eat because I was growing, and I tried hard to do what he said.

Remedios came in from the market carrying baskets of fruit and vegetables. I asked her why she didn't let Maria do the shopping, and she said that we couldn't let the servants know that we ate more fruit and vegetables during Passover because we couldn't eat grains.

We didn't eat bread on the eve of the holiday or on the days that followed. Mother served cakes she baked from unleavened white wheat, and Juan said that he wanted to eat those white cakes all the time, instead of bread. But on the sixth day of the holiday, he asked for real bread!

The Easter prayer in our church was very festive. All the boys came dressed in the clothes we were going to wear in the processions: a white shirt and a black tunic. And there were bouquets of flowers everywhere.

In Padre Pedro's sermon, he talked about the greatness of Christianity, the only religion that could save humanity. But only on the condition that everyone believed in it and there were no more wicked heretics like the *judaizantes*, whose vile behavior desecrated the holy cross and prevented our salvation.

As I walked in the procession, carrying on my shoulders the platform depicting the crucifixion of Jesus, I didn't look at the enormous crowds that filled the streets and watched us from their balconies and windows. I kept my eyes on the ground, feeling as if my back were being crushed under the heavy weight.

How long would we have to keep doing this, I thought, dressing and acting like Christians when in our hearts, we believed in our true religion, the Torah of Moses?

After Easter, Antonio started teaching us again. He looked happy, and it was obvious how much he wanted to be here. And Juan was especially happy on the day Antonio came back. I wasn't happy or sorry. I was indifferent about our lessons. All I wanted was to study more science and less theology. My excuse was that I wanted to try and learn theology myself to see whether

I could do it.

Every once in a while, Antonio left the study room and went into the living room. I knew he was looking for Remedios, but I didn't tell him that she was at Aunt Tereza's house.

Finally, I heard him ask Juan about our sister, and my little brother said that as far as he knew from our parents, Remedios was taking care of our sick aunt.

A day or two after that, Antonio asked me what illness my aunt had, because he'd seen her in church and she looked healthy.

"She only looks healthy," I replied. "And she's not allowed to know how sick she is. She has a very serious disease, and we're all praying to the Holy Mother to help her!"

I didn't know why, but my relationship with Antonio wasn't as friendly as it used to be a few months ago. It was as if there were a wall between us. Almost the only thing we talked about now was my studies.

But it was Antonio who told me about the upcoming trial of Leonor, Violanti's sister, and her husband, Shimon Prados.

I must have gotten pale when I heard this, because Antonio said in a worried tone, "You don't know those people, do you?"

I shook my head.

"You only knew the girl's family, isn't that right?"

I nodded.

"Do they still live across the way?"

"I don't think so. I haven't seen them for a long time," I replied.

"Where are they?"

"Who knows and who cares?" I said, trying to sound indifferent.

"But Juan tells me that their younger daughter, Violanti, is in love with you."

"Come on, Antonio. You know Juan. He makes things up. He's a child. He tells stories about everyone!"

Antonio looked at me hard when he heard that. "About everyone?" I knew what he was waiting for, but I didn't say anything.

"Santiago's friends say that he's sure about how the trial will end—that girl won't be a wife to her husband or to anyone else. The fire will consume her!"

I looked at Antonio, stunned. I never expected to hear him say anything like that. And definitely not in that gloating tone.

"When will they have the *auto de fe*?" I asked after a long silence

"They say it'll be soon. The husband and wife have been in prison for a few weeks. Their property has been confiscated and people say they don't have a chance anymore."

Not many days after that conversation, I found out that not only Antonio but other people who knew the accused couple even slightly were taking an interest in their case. All of Seville was waiting for the *auto de fe* that would soon take place .

Chapter Seventeen
THE PRADOS TRIAL

The summer of 1636, when the Prados trial was held, was blazing hot. I'd never suffered from the heat as much as I did that summer. At noon, when the sun was at its zenith, I felt as if fire were falling from the sky and burning the city. Maybe that was Seville's punishment for the terrible torture that Leonor and her husband endured in the cellars of the Triana Fortress, I thought.

The people who were going to burn Leonor and Shimon Prados at the stake because of their religious beliefs—and the only charge against them was that they obeyed the commandments of the Torah of Moses— were the ones who deserved to burn in the fires of hell. That's what I thought. I was sure that the terrible heat in Seville was a reminder to the Inquisitors that they were flesh and blood too, that they—if they made a mistake—could also be sent to hell.

Everyone in Seville was talking about the *auto de fe* that would soon take place outside the St. Paul Dominican Church, and I don't think anyone doubted that Leonor and her husband would be burned at the stake. The rumor was spreading that they were tortured and had confessed, and they hadn't recanted or asked for forgiveness.

Everyone talked about them with anger. They said they were the source of all the evil in the world. They said that because of them and people like them, there were plagues and poverty.

Everywhere Father went, people talked to him about those *marranos* who were standing trial. Sometimes, when he came home, he couldn't keep it in and he'd tell us what he heard about the trial.

But we rarely saw Father at home during the last few months, and Mother had started going out more often too.

Many times, I asked why they were going out so much and staying away so long, but the only answers I got were meant to keep me from worrying.

"Don't worry, Manuel, we'll try to come home soon," that's more or less what my parents told me when I asked where they were going.

During the hottest hours of the day, we stayed in the house and studied. But sometimes, when Antonio came early in the morning, we went out to walk around the city with him. Antonio used lots of tricks to get me to tell him Aunt Tereza's address, but I never went near her house with him. And Juan had sworn—without knowing why—not to tell anyone where our Aunt and Uncle lived. I remember that Juan was very surprised when Father made him swear, and the first thing he said was, "But we can tell Antonio, can't we?" And Father replied gravely, "You swore an oath not to tell anyone, no one at all. Remember that, Juan!"

On our walks, we saw the preparations the city was making for the *auto de fe:* fixing the roads and strengthening the bridge over the Guadalquivir. Antonio said that thousands of people would come to see the sentences carried out, not only for the Prados but for all of the others who stood accused and convicted. We also saw lots of soldiers who had been brought to Seville to keep order during the *auto de fe.*

Indictments had already been handed down against Leonor and her husband. A prosecutor and a defense lawyer had been appointed, and a date had been set for hearing their evidence. Except for Santiago, many people had spoken on Leonor's behalf. Violanti's sister was very well liked. But would those testimonies help her?

I asked Father about that, and he said that he thought the testimonies accusing her would hold more weight. Not only that, but everyone in the city knew that the young couple themselves had confessed to committing the crimes they'd been accused of.

I'd never been inside the Triana Fortress and I did not know much about how the trials were conducted there. All we knew was that the judges had consulted with many experts before passing sentence.

On the day when the verdicts would be handed down, the day of the *auto de fe,* crowds swarmed to St. Paul's Church in Seville. Many people had come from other cities, and the streets were bursting with them. Soldiers directed the wagons so they wouldn't block the way to the church.

At six in the morning, there was already a tumult in the streets because the accused were taken out of the

Triana Fortress and paraded to the church. There were a lot of other prisoners besides the Prados, and the long procession—surrounded by soldiers—trailed slowly through the streets.

All the accused were wearing *sambenitos*, the special robe for people being sentenced by the Inquisition, and they stumbled along the streets. Their feet had been crushed during torture. They were led to the stage that had been built in front of the church, and when they were standing in their places, the Grand Inquisitor of the Triana Fortress began his sermon.

I was there. People would have been suspicious if we hadn't come. I kept thinking about Violanti, that maybe she would come in disguise and I would be the only one who recognized her.

I saw Leonor, Violanti's sister. The torture hadn't made her clear face less beautiful, and it was flooded by a strange kind of light. But the sight of her husband's face, red and swollen from torture, scared me so much that I couldn't look at him.

And I didn't hear even one word of the Inquisitor's sermon.

Even though the crowd gathered in front of the church was enormous, there was silence during the sermon. We were standing close to the stage—the Duke, who was Father's patient, had gotten us good places.

There was a loud cry in the middle of the sermon— a woman wearing a black *sambenito* collapsed. How hot they must be in those coarse robes, I thought pityingly.

Two guards hurried over to the woman lying on the floor and picked her up. Then the Inquisitor went back to his sermon. When he finished, the verdicts were read. Each prisoner whose name was called stepped forward and stood at attention. The first one to be called was the woman who had fallen. The guards supported her so she wouldn't fall again.

The Inquisitor read her sentence: life imprisonment in a tiny dungeon.

When the woman wearing the black *sambenito* was taken away, a young man in a light-colored *sambenito* was called, and he received the same sentence as the woman before him.

After the verdict was read, he kneeled down at the Inquisitor's feet and thanked him. Then he was taken away.

Leonor Prados was the fifth one to have her sentence read. I stopped breathing and listened to every word. "The accused, Leonor Prados, née de Govilla, confessed to obeying the commandments of the Hebrew religion, and she is sentenced to five years imprisonment in the Triana Fortress. The bones of her mother-in-law, Juana, née Versano, who led her daughter-in-law astray, will be removed from the grave and burned at the stake."

Leonor kneeled in front of the Inquisitor and was taken away by the guards. Then her husband, Shimon Prados, was brought forward to hear his sentence.

"Shimon Prados is accused of desecrating the holy cross." Angry murmurs buzzed through the crowd. When there was silence again, the Inquisitor continued. "The accused confessed that he does not believe in our holy Messiah and that he follows the commandments of

the Hebrew religion." The frightening murmur buzzed through the crowd again, and it took a while for it to die down. "Therefore," the Inquisitor went on, "and since the accused does not wish to refrain from his evil deeds and does not ask for forgiveness, the Holy Court of the Inquisition sentences him to be burned alive. . . " Before the Inquisitor could finish speaking, a huge roar burst from the mob. "Long live the holy Inquisition!"

Everyone was overjoyed. People jumped up and down and hugged each other. The noise was deafening. I stood closer to Father and Juan, and Mother and Remedios moved closer to us too. If I hadn't been standing there with my family, I think I would have fainted from fright and horror.

It took a while for things to quiet down. Sentences were read again, and the prisoners kneeled and gave thanks for the mercy they'd been shown.

Shimon Prados was the only one who didn't kneel. Even that evening, when they lit a pile of dry branches under him, the man did not utter a sound. If he had said something, we would have heard it. There was a deathly silence in the church square until his flesh caught fire. Only when the flames began licking his flesh did the crowd let out an enormous cheer and the festivities began.

The mob stayed to celebrate in the church square and the neighboring streets. We made our way through the crowd, trying not to get separated from each other. We didn't get home until late, stunned and dazed.

We hadn't put anything in our mouths all day except for water, which we'd taken with us in leather bags. The servants naturally stayed near the church to celebrate the *auto de fe*. And Mother didn't ask if we were hungry. I thought that it would take a long time before I could swallow any food after what we went through that day, and I was sure that the rest of my family felt the same way.

We bathed and went to bed.

I woke up before dawn to the sound of a scream that came from my mouth while I was asleep. I remembered my dream and understood why I screamed. Everything I'd seen at the *auto de fe* had come back to me in the dream, but now I didn't hold in my feelings. Tears sprang to my eyes and flowed without a stop. Even though I thought I was acting like a child, I didn't try to stop the crying. It felt good, and I cried until the tears dried up.

Then I got up. I washed my face with cold water from the jug and went into the living room. I sat down on the couch and tried to organize my thoughts, which were all muddled. I asked myself questions. Why did that happen to Shimon Prados and where did he get the strength to endure it? And how can people be happy about watching someone burn? And what will happen to us if they find out we're Jewish? And where is Violanti?

Just thinking about her made me get up and go to the window. I pushed aside the curtain and my breath caught—there was a faint light in the window across the way. Was I mistaken?

Of course I was. They can't be back. I'm hallucinating.

And when I strained my eyes to see better, I could tell that the window was dark. I just imagined that there was light, I thought. And at that moment, I heard a noise, and very slowly, the window across the way opened and a head peeked out. I saw two braids hanging from it, and I could barely keep from shouting, "Violanti, Violanti!"

I whispered her name and she heard me. If I only had wings to fly to her, to her window.

She signaled me with her hand to go out to the alley. As if my wish had been granted and I'd grown invisible wings, I flew, I floated, and there I was, in the alley, waiting for her.

I was so excited that I couldn't say a word, and she couldn't speak either. We just held hands tightly.

We didn't go far. Sounds of the mob celebrating still came from the city. We sat at the end of the alley, and Violanti told me where she'd been hiding and the hell she'd been through since we last saw each other. Then we talked about the trial.

"My sister Leonor was very brave during the torture," she said in a trembling voice. "She denied that we, her family, were faithful to the commandments of Moses. She said she hadn't known anything about the Hebrew religion until she got married. She learned everything from her husband's mother when she married him. Her mother-in-law, who died a year ago, saved her by dying and that's how we were saved too.

"And Shimon Prados, my brother-in-law, was a hero too," Violanti said, weeping. "He'd loved Leonor since he was a child. But she didn't love him. She fell in love with a Christian . . ."

"Yes, I met Santiago," I told Violanti when she stopped crying.

"If only my parents had been able to carry out their plan before Santiago found Leonor, none of this would have happened."

"What plan?"

"Ever since my parents found out that Leonor and Santiago loved each other, and that was about two years ago, they've been trying to find a ship and arrange for us and some other families of New Christians to leave Spain. That's why they went to Cádiz, Málaga, and other cities and left me alone so much. They were looking for *conversos* who wanted to run away with us, who had enough money to hire a ship with us. But it's so hard to get into contact with people like that. Look, even though we're neighbors, I wasn't sure you were a Hebrew like me. And you didn't think I was one either.

"My parents were in great danger, and they were almost turned over to the authorities. It was in Málaga. The talked to a family they thought were like us, and it turned out that they were pure Christians. Luckily for us, someone warned my parents, and they managed to get away before anyone found out who they were.

"Now, my parents have found a ship owner who is also a New Christian and is willing to take us to Amsterdam. There the Jews are not persecuted and we can follow the commandments of our Torah openly. My older brother, who lives in Málaga, wants to come with us. And my sister Rosana, who lives in Granada, plans to joins us with her husband and daughter. And there are a few other families who want to leave with us. We still don't have enough money for the ship, but my parents say that we'll be able to raise it.

"The problem now is Leonor—they can't leave while she's still a prisoner in the Triana Fortress!"

What Violanti told me about her parents traveling all over Spain to find *conversos* and raise money to escape made me think about my own parents. They'd been away from home so often and wouldn't tell me why. Did they have a plan like the one Violanti had just told me about? Were my parents planning to leave Spain so they could separate Remedios and Antonio? After all, they couldn't hide my sister in Aunt Tereza's house forever!

I told Violanti what I was thinking, and she said, "There's no reason anymore for our parents not to talk openly. You can leave, and you should, especially because of Remedios's relationship with your teacher. I tried to warn her through you. I saw how much our family suffered because of Leonor and Santiago, and I wanted to save your family from going through the same thing. Somehow, I knew from the first day you came to the neighborhood that you were Hebrews like us. But I wasn't absolutely sure until you told me," Violanti said.

"I told my parents about you," she continued. "And because we can't sail on the ship my parents hired, at least all their efforts won't be for nothing if you and your family leave Spain on it."

"No, Violanti, I won't leave Spain without you," I said, and she put her hand on my mouth.

"Ssh, Manuel. It's dawn already and people are starting to wake up. Let's go home now so our parents won't see that we've gone and won't worry about us."

Chapter Eighteen
AN OLD FRIEND
RETURNS

At the meeting between my parents and Violanti's, it turned out that my parents did have a similar plan. They planned to leave Spain with some other New Christian families. But they thought they'd do it by land: travel by wagon to Bordeaux and from there by sea to Amsterdam, which was known to be an enlightened city. But now, hearing what Violanti's parents had to say, my parents changed their complicated plan and accepted the de Govilla's suggestion to travel on the ship they'd hired because the owner, who was a *converso*, could be trusted.

The next few days were taken up with secret preparations for the journey. Our parents were away from home more than ever, but that didn't bother me anymore. At first, we thought that Aunt Catalina and Uncle Alonso, together with Mencia and Fernando, would be coming with us. But in the end, they couldn't because of Uncle Alonso's business. Aunt Tereza and Uncle Lorenzo decided not to sail with us either because Federico still had another year before he graduated from Alcalá de Henares University. But all of our relatives said they would eventually follow us.

For the time being, we didn't tell Juan anything about the plan to get out of Spain. As for Remedios— she knew. My parents told her and didn't hide the reason. But I didn't know how she took the news because I hardly ever saw her. She was still staying with Aunt Tereza and Uncle Lorenzo.

We continued studying with Antonio until one morning when he pulled up in a wagon dressed in traveling clothes. "I'm sorry to leave you this way," he said, "but I was offered a teaching position at Osona University and I am on my way there now."

He left a letter for Father explaining his reason for leaving, and a letter for Remedios. She wouldn't tell us what it said.

Juan cried when Antonio climbed onto the wagon, and I suddenly felt affection for that nice young teacher I'd spent so many hours with.

From the wagon, Antonio waved to us with one hand and wiped his eyes with the other.

When I told Violanti that Antonio had gone, she smiled and said, "If so, then it isn't so urgent for your family to leave Spain now." Naturally, I agreed with her.

But my parents continued the preparations, and I felt that every minute I spent away from Violanti was wasted. So we were together from morning till night, and those were the most wonderful days of my life. One morning, when Violanti and I were out walking, we met Lopez's gang.

Pasqual was excited to see me, and he shook Violanti's hand warmly. Lopez was friendly too, but seemed.

Tomas whispered to Miguel, and I heard him say, "That's the witch's sister."

"They're both Jewish converts. Their time will come too," one of them said. Was it Miguel? I wondered, but didn't turn around to see.

Violanti and I walked a lot, and one day, without planning it, we found ourselves standing in front the Triana Fortress.

The wall kept us from seeing what was going on inside. We walked all around it, and when we came back to the gate, Violanti sighed and said, "I would give anything to see Leonor. I would do anything . . ."

"Maybe we could ask the commander of the Fortress?" I suggested.

Violanti dismissed the idea with a wave of her hand, and her face filled with sadness. "My parents already asked him, and he said that we had to send a letter of request to the *Suprema*, but it takes a long time to get an answer."

Violanti was still speaking when a boy riding a donkey came out of the Fortress gates. I looked at him in surprise and rubbed my eyes.

"Aldino?" I shouted.

The boy stopped the donkey. He looked at me for a while, and when he remembered he jumped off the donkey and came over to hug me. "Manuel! Is it really you?"

That meeting was so unexpected that we didn't know what to say.

"I never thought I'd see you again," Aldino said,

finally breaking the silence. "It feels like ten years have gone by since that day you came to hide under the tree near the river."

"And you, Aldino, gave me some delicious cheese to eat."

"The black sheep that gave us the milk for cheese is dead," Aldino said, his expression turning sad. "A disaster happened to us, a terrible disaster."

"Yes, my father told me. We weren't in Seville during the epidemic, but my father was, and he saw the monks take you and your brother."

"They took my brother to be a servant for a *regidor* in Toledo, and they put me to work here in the fortress. Who's she?" he asked, pointing to Violanti. "Your sister?"

When I said no and introduced Violanti, Aldino's black eyes seemed to get blacker and his sad face looked pained. He shook her hand and said, "I'm so sorry about your brother-in-law. Shimon Prados was the bravest man I've ever seen, and I feel so bad about your sister, who's a prisoner here in the fortress. Sometimes they send me to bring her food and water, but she returns the plate still full, and I've heard her crying many times."

Violanti's face turned pale. I went over to her. I wanted to cheer her up, to comfort, to soothe her, but I didn't know how.

"Her parents sent a request to the *Suprema* in Madrid. They asked permission to visit her," I told Aldino, "but they still haven't gotten an answer."

The sound of steps coming from the fortress drove

the three of us away from the gate we were standing near. Aldino's donkey refused to run, and he had to pull it along with him.

We saw a group of people leaving the monastery, and Aldino hopped onto the back of his donkey and said, "You shouldn't be seen here. Come tomorrow at the same time and we'll try to figure out what to do. Wait for me on the other side of the wall."

We didn't stay to see whether the people stopped next to Aldino or passed right by him. We hurried away so they wouldn't see us from the fortress, and we kept on running almost all the way home.

I felt like I was running on air, as if I had a reason to be happy. Was it because I'd seen Aldino? I asked myself.

Not far from the alley where Violanti and I lived, we stopped, panting from the run.

"Manuel, do you think that boy you know will help us?" Violanti asked.

"I'm sure he'll try. He has a good heart, and even though I don't know him well, I consider him my friend," I replied.

"If only we could see my sister secretly, I wouldn't ask for anything more," Violanti said, touching her chin with the tips of her fingers and looking up as if she were praying.

That evening, we weren't sad when we said good-night. Most of our partings were sad, even when they were only for a few hours. But that evening, we parted with hearts full of anticipation for our meeting with Aldino.

But the next day we were bitterly disappointed. We waited a long time at the wall, where Aldino said we should wait, but he didn't come. We looked for him over the next few days too, but he wasn't there.

Meanwhile, preparations for the journey were almost finished. There were enough passengers and they'd raised enough money. My parents told the servants that we were going on a trip and would be away for more than two months, at least. They also told that to Juan, and asked him to pack his textbooks and clothes.

My brother was very excited about the "trip." It never entered his mind that we were running away from Spain and would never come back.

My uncles, Alonso and Lorenzo, said they would sell our property after we left and help us with many other things.

We were all tense and didn't speak very much, except for Juan, who talked constantly about the "trip", and none of us, except Juan, showed any signs of happiness. My parents were worried about the danger of getting caught. We knew about other ships that had been stopped by the authorities and all the passengers had been arrested.

We knew that the Inquisition sent secret agents to the ports to see who was boarding the ships and whether there were New Christian families among them who planned to emigrate to countries where they could practice the religion of their forefathers.

Remedios must have had reasons of her own to be sad, because I hadn't seen a smile on her face for months.

As for me, if Violanti had been coming with us, I would've been the happiest person in the whole world. But there didn't seem to be any chance that would happen. The de Govilla family wouldn't leave Spain while Leonor was imprisoned in the fortress. Even so, Violanti's brother and his family decided to join us, and her married sister, along with her husband and daughter, was thinking of sailing with us too.

I begged Violanti, "Please, please come with your brother and maybe your other sister will come too. You could be with them!"

But she said she wouldn't leave without her parents and Leonor.

"Leonor will be in prison for five years," I reminded Violanti. "You'll have to wait five years for her!"

She asked me not to make it harder for her by saying those things, and I had to do what she asked. We only had a few days left to spend together, and I wanted them to be good days, even though we were sad about having to say good-bye soon.

Early one morning, three days before we were supposed to sail, someone pulled the bell. Maria opened the door and, with a strange expression on her face, came to tell me that a Moorish boy was looking for me.

I almost didn't recognize Aldino in the robe he was wearing as a disguise. He spoke very quickly, telling me that there was only one way Leonor's family could see her, and that was to get her out of the fortress. He said he could do that, but only on the condition that we could find a safe place for her right away.

"How dangerous would that be for you?" I asked him.

"I'm not afraid for myself," Aldino replied. "Just the opposite. If I can get Leonor de Govilla out of prison, I'll be settling a score I have with the fortress. They make me do so many things there that I don't want to do!"

"You don't want to stay in the fortress?"

"They make me do things that I hate, and they threaten never to let me see my brother again if I don't do them. If I wasn't afraid that they'd do something bad to him, I'd run away. The least I can do is help your girlfriend's sister escape," Aldino said quickly. "I have to go back. If I don't, they'll punish me!"

"Punish you, Aldino?"

"I couldn't come to meet you near the wall because they punished me. They wouldn't let me out of my room for more than a week. And only because they saw me talking to you."

"Then we better hurry," I said, and we went out into the alley.

We went to Violanti's house and Aldino told Violanti and her parents all the details of his escape plan for Leonor.

Three days and a night had passed since then, and we weren't in Seville anymore. We were standing on the deck of the ship surrounded by quiet. All we could hear was the whisper of the waves.

Violanti was standing next to me on the deck. I could feel her shivering.

"If Leonor doesn't come," she said, "my parents and I will get into a small boat and go back to shore."

I knew we couldn't wait too long. The captain said it was very dangerous to be sitting there, not far from the shore. He said we'd only wait a little while longer, and if the boat we were waiting for didn't come, he'd pick up anchor and we'd sail out to sea.

We looked north, straining our eyes to see. And suddenly I started to get very excited. Weren't those oars rowing in the foam? Was that a boat leaving a silver trail behind it?

Violanti's hand shook in mine.

"I see them," she whispered. "It's my sister."

We saw a figure climbing the rope ladder, and the boat moved away from the ship. I waved to Aldino, but he was rowing quickly and probably didn't see me.

Leonor's parents reached out to help her onto the deck, and I saw her fall into their arms.

"I'm so happy, Manuel," Violanti said in a trembling voice.

I held her hand and said, "From now on, I'm not Manuel. Now I can call myself by my real name. Emmanuel."

GLOSSARY

amidah prayer: the Jewish standing prayer having eighteen blessings

amigos: friends

auto de fe: an Inquisition Act of Faith, in which convicted people were burned at the stake in front of large crowds

borceguinero: sandal maker

buenas tardes: good afternoon

buenos días: good day or hello

capa: cape, or tunic

chiquito: little boy

conversos: converts to Christianity

cristianos nuevos: a term applied to Jews and Moors who were converted to Christianity

Gospels: books of the New Testament

gracias: thank you

guardas: policemen

Inquisitors: Inquisition investigators

judaizantes: Jews who had converted to Christianity

limpieza certificate: a document testifying that a person has had pure Christian blood for generations

mañana: tomorrow

marranos: literally meaning swine, the term was applied to the descendants of baptized Jews suspected of secret adherence to Judaism

meravedís: unit of money

mitzvah: a Jewish commandment; also a good deed

morisco: Muslim (Moorish) forced converts to Christianity

¿qué tal?: What's up?

real: unit of money

regidores: city councilmen

sambenito: robe worn by people on trial during the Inquisition

Santo Oficio: the Holy Office of the Inquisition

shma Yisrael: Jewish statement of belief

sí, sí: yes, yes

sucios: swine

sukkah, sukkot (plural): hut(s) prepared outdoors for the Sukkot festival

Sukkot: the Festival of Booths in which Jews reside in a three-sided structure known as a sukkah for eight days

Suprema: the Supreme Court of the Inquisition in Madrid

Torre del Oro: Tower of Gold

HISTORICAL AFTERWORD

The Spanish Inquisition was established in 1478 by King Ferdinand and Queen Isabella to enforce devotion to the Catholic Church in Spain.

In 1492, the King and Queen ordered the expulsion of all Jews and Moors from Spain and all of its kingdoms. Both groups were given the choice of accepting conversion to Christianity or leaving the country. The exact numbers are not known, but it is estimated that as many as half of Spain's 200,000 Jews chose to adopt Christianity in order to remain in their homeland. These converts became known as *conversos*, or New Christians. Of those who fled, many went to Portugal—where the Inquisition followed them in 1532, thus forcing them to become *conversos* after all.

Spain's Inquisition had jurisdiction over baptized Christians—which included the Jews and Moors who chose to convert to Christianity rather than be expelled. Queen Isabella had heard rumors of false converts among the Jews who had recently converted to Catholicism. These *conversos* became primary targets of the Inquisitors.

To carry out the mandate of the Inquisition, a tribunal, or committee, would convene in a city or town. (Seville was one of the first locations.) Those citizens under suspicion of disloyalty to the Catholic Church would be called in for questioning. This often led to an *auto de fe,* an Act of Faith. At this public ceremony, a reaffirmation of faith was either accepted or the individual was accused of heresy (rejection of the church by a baptized member). Clergymen presided at these proceedings and delivered the punishments, which included confinement to dungeons, torture, or death.

Conversos endured the most intense persecution through 1530. However, in the early seventeenth century, when our story takes place, the Portuguese Inquisition was even more ruthless than Spain's, so many Portuguese *conversos* at that time fled to Spain. This resulted in an increase in the investigations of *conversos,* many of whom, like the Nuñez family, had been recognized as Christians for many generations.

Although the intensity fluctuated, the work of the Inquisition continued for many generations. Eventually, the Age of Enlightenment influenced the people of Spain to rethink their beliefs about the roles of religion and government, leading to the end of the Inquisition in 1834.